UNSPEAKABLE RITES

AN ALKEMYA NOVELLA

CLINT WESTGARD

ALSO BY CLINT WESTGARD

Alkemya Universe:

Unspeakable Rites

The Shadow Men:

> *Realm of Shadows*
>
> *Council of Shadows*
>
> *Dance of Shadows*

The Sojourners Cycle:

> *The Forgotten*
>
> *The Apostate*
>
> The Acolyte (forthcoming)
>
> The Double (forthcoming)
>
> The Sojourner (forthcoming)

The Maleficio Chronicles

The Trials of the Minotaur

Published by Lost Quarter Books
www.lostquarterbooks.com

This edition 2017

Cover image: © Elen | Dreamstime.com

ISBN: 978-1-928035-31-2

For Ursula Le Guin, for all her inspiration.

CONTENTS

ONE:

AN INVESTIGATION

THE STORM SWEPT through the city of Tson in the middle of the night as most everyone slept, leaving in its calamitous path a sea of fallen branches, and not a few fallen trees, along with a seemingly endless amount of unidentifiable refuse, mostly stolen from shacks in the poorest quarters. Many of those did not survive the tempest and the next morning the streets of these quarters were filled with those who had been left homeless. Mixed in amongst all this detritus on one street near the city wall was the body of a young man. The local Magistery discovered it on their patrols of the neighborhood and had the body taken to the central mortuary.

Because of the youth's shade, the Magistery notified the Chaziqs of the Enir Quarter in the hopes that they would know if one of their community had gone missing. Dutifully, the four men put on their finest robes and made their way to the central mortuary to look upon the body, all of them declaring that they did not know the man and that he was not from their quarter.

Chief Magister Gahryll a Tyranil frowned and pursed his lips. He ran a distracted hand over his head and the close-cropped hair there, a habit he had formed once he had started going bald several years before. Each time he did it, he was left annoyed at the fact there was less and less to pass his hand through, to say nothing of the fact that what remained was turning grey. All artifacts of his advancing years, but not so advanced yet, as he never failed to remind himself.

He forced his thoughts back to the matter at hand. There were not many Enir in Tson, so it was not unusual to expect the Chaziqs to know the majority of them. It was strange as well that no word had gone among their people of someone missing a son or a brother.

"You will ask around for me with your people," Gahryll said. "Perhaps he is new to the city."

Reluctantly, or so it seemed to Gahryll, the Chaziqs agreed to this request. He did not give much thought to their hesitation. It was just a dead itinerant after all, and an Enir at that, hardly worth wasting any thought over. There were more pressing concerns at hand.

The Golden Veil had recently returned from beneath the smoldering ruins they had left ten years before, striking at the Gver of Lastl during the Gver's Council in Cratiol. Rumors of their resurrection had gone wild throughout the Realm of Craitol, no doubt attracting disaffected nobles of rank to their banner in every city and town. With the coming war against the Shadow Men bringing the absence of Gver Hythel and his finest cohorts of men from Tson, malcontents like those in Veil would see an opportunity to strike, which meant that Magistery would need to be watchful. Something like this death of a youth of no account could only distract from their true duty, to protect the city.

No word came back from the Chaziqs, and Gahryll had his assistant Ducaryh—a man of Kragian extraction, but of unquestionable competence—arrange to have the body put on display in the public room of the mortuary where anyone in the city could look upon it. The dead displayed there were sometimes identified and claimed, but as most came from the vagrant classes—prostitutes and homeless, thieves and murderers, or the poorest of the Realm, cast from the countryside into the city in the vain hope of shaping a new life—this was exceedingly rare.

The youth was evidently one of these sorts, with no kin looking for him, for in the three days that his body was displayed no one stepped forward to claim it. While this was ongoing, Gahryll ordered a cursory investigation be conducted by one of the Magisters. The man assigned to the task, Mihiubel a Jorhkah, was extremely thorough, though, and when he brought his report to Gahryll, he indicated his belief that the youth had died at the hands of another and that further investigation was warranted.

"You don't think the storm killed him?" Gahryll said. They were sitting across from each other in his offices in the Magisterium. "It was quite violent. If he was left outdoors, it could easily have done him in."

"No, Nes Gahryll," Mihiubel said, with a firm shake of his head. "Did you notice his robes? Very fine silk, too fine for anyone forced to live on the street. No, I am quite certain he was living somewhere, but it was not anywhere near where he was found."

"What makes you say that?"

"For starters, it is a poor neighborhood. Most of the inhabitants could not dream of owning such robes. And no one remembers him. I went to the Enir Quarter as well, thinking he must have lived somewhere there, no matter what the Chaziqs told you. But it seems not. They are all quite adamant. Very strange. I found a few who recognize him though, but they will not admit it."

This attracted Gahryll's attention. "Why not?"

Mihiubel held out his hands. "I can't say. No one will speak to me of it. Except one man who said he thought he recalled seeing him coming and going from a particular house."

Something about his phrasing of those last words drew the Chief Magister's attention. "What particular kind of house?"

"It is an academy, I believe, though I haven't called on them yet. I imagine he was in service there in some form, or servicing the trulls."

"So call on them and see if there is someone there who wishes to take possession of the body and let us be done with this matter."

"There is something else," Mihiubel said. "I took the liberty of removing his robes. I'm sure you noted the bruises upon his face. His chest is similarly bruised. And there are lacerations as well, on both his chest and his back. Symbols of some sort."

"Were they enough to kill him?"

Mihiubel shook his head. "I think not. None of his wounds were severe. If I were to guess, I would say they were symbols for some kind of rites."

Gahryll nodded. It was all very curious and he could see why Mihiubel was drawn to the case, but in the end he could see no reason to pursue the matter with so many other concerns at hand. If the youth had been murdered, as the Magister believed, there was little to be done about it. Not with the Enir Quarter refusing to help and no witnesses to the crime, or obvious suspects. The Enir punish their own, he told himself, and that seemed as satisfactory an explanation as any. The youth had crossed someone, perhaps at the academy, perhaps elsewhere, and had paid the price.

With no one to claim the body after four days on display, Gahryll sent word to the Chaziqs to dispose of the corpse as per their customs. The Enir buried their dead and presumably would want to see this one interred, lest they anger their ancestors. It was Mihiubel who brought word that the Chaziqs had refused to honor the body.

"Well have it burned then," Gahryll said, with a shake of his head.

Mihiubel nodded, but did not leave the room. "You don't find it odd that they are refusing. Have you ever heard of such a thing? An Enir risking the wrath of their ancestors by refusing to bury one of their own. The whole Quarter could be cursed."

"The Gods curse them already, what does it matter if their ancestors do as well?"

"I just think we should find out what this youth has done that would have them cast him out so completely. There is only one thing I can think of that might lead them to do that."

"What is that?" Gahryll said, his mind already on the papers Ducaryh had brought him to sign. Orders and reports and messages. There was so much to attend to and it was already afternoon.

"Perhaps he has been playing at alkemya," Mihiubel said.

That did get Gahryhll's attention. An Enir practicing alkemya was unheard of. They abhorred the art. It was condemned by their ceinobytes and cursed by their ancestors. Any Enir who did so would know he was crossing to a realm from which there was no return. He would be an Enir no longer.

Gahryll also knew that no Council Adepts would ever train an Enir. There was only one kind of alkemyst who would dare to, and the Chief Magister thought he had done with them long ago. Apparently not, for it seemed there were Desecrators in Tson.

Desecrators and the Veil. Was it ten years ago? No, then he would be in Haigah Pass watching the best of his generation perish. He shook his head, lost in the thought, before looking up at Mihiubel.

"You think we should pay a visit to this academy then, I take it?"

Mihiubel nodded and with a sigh of annoyance Gahryll rose to join him.

They went to one of the finer streets of the Enir Quarter where a number of the leading families had their trading houses, some of them even affiliated with the great houses of the Enir Republics. Trading was what the Enir were known for, of course, that and their mercenaries. An untold amount of coin was being spent now by the Qraul of Craitol on cohorts of mercenaries from the Republics to wage his war against the Shadow Men. An utter waste of coin by any measure of the cloth, Gahryll thought, but was sensible enough not to say aloud.

Mihiubel led him to a house that stood out among all the others on the street for being drab looking and small by comparison. They entered and were immediately greeted by a youth, so fine featured and pretty, that Gahryll at first glance mistook him for a girl. His skin had a hint of the olive green shade of the Enir, but otherwise he was as ghostly as a Kragian, with their reddish black hair and dark, depthless eyes.

The youth went paler than his shade at the sight of them and he bowed deeply. "Magisters, such an honor to welcome you here. I will summon the lady of the house."

"See that you do," Gahryll said, summoning as much ice to his tone as he could. Mihiubel, for his part, seemed unperturbed to find himself in such a place and cast his eyes about at the walls, admiring the tapestries there.

Gahryll turned his attention there as well and was horrified to see depictions of men in various states of congress with one another. "Did the Enir happen to mention the kind of academy this was?"

Mihiubel shook his head. "No, I took the liberty of speaking with some others about this house, without mentioning the youth. They had some interesting things to say."

Gahryll frowned. "And what would that be?"

"That men here from across the city practice dark arts."

"Of that there can be little doubt," Gahryll said. He had to resist the urge to brush clean his robes, not wanting to display just how uncomfortable he was. "Everything that occurs here goes against all the Gods have taught us."

Mihiubel did not reply and the youth returned with an Enir woman, of indeterminate age, wearing a vibrant red wig, her green shade lightened with paint.

"Magisters," she said in a brusque tone, as she bowed to each of them. "I presume this is not a social call."

"It is certainly not," Gahryll said. "I am the Chief Magister of this city and this is Magister Mihiubel. We are investigating the death of an Enir youth from last week. He died the night of the storm."

"I see, Magisters," the woman said in a neutral tone, her eyes darting from face to face.

"I was told he was seen attending here," Mihiubel said, and proceeded to describe the youth and his dress.

The woman hesitated and Gahryll said, "I do not need to remind you that a word from me can close this establishment. Be grateful I have not done so already."

"There is no need to close us," the woman said.

"Mind your tongue," Gahryll said. "Or I will see that it absents you. I can see reason enough to tear this building to its foundations standing right before me. What goes on here goes against the Gods."

"There is a house like this in every quarter of this city, Chief Magister," the woman said. "Will you close them too, or will the Enir be the only people to feel the wrath of the Magistery?"

"Perhaps it would be best to attend to the matter at hand for now," Mihiubel said with a calm smile. "The rest can be dealt with later if it need be."

Gahryll gave a curt nod and looked to the woman who composed her expression. "Isahem did attend here," she said. "He was with us for nearly a year and a half."

"And what can you tell us about him?" Gahryll said.

"I do not inquire into the past of those here," the woman said.

"I was told that Isahem might be involved in some dark practices of a different sort," Mihiubel said. "That such things took place here as well."

"I don't know what you are referring to," the woman said.

"He is referring to alkemya, in particular that practiced by the Desecrators," Gahryll said, wielding his words as though they were a spear and she a beast he was trying to gore.

The woman's face darkened with anger. "What do you take us for Chief Magister? No Enir would forsake their ancestors and their soul for your cursed arts."

"It seems to me you have forsaken all else," Gahryll said.

The woman's lips trembled as she fought to hold her tongue, but she was unable to, the damn bursting and unleashing a torrent. "It is you Craitolians and your Adepts who have forsaken all. Going into the desert to fight the cursed Shadows, all over alkemya. What would your Gods say to that? And you cannot pretend with me. I know your kind. You come in here holding your nose and making a show of being appalled at what goes on behind these doors. But when you go home, you have no problem going to all fours."

She continued on after that, but Gahryll did not hear her. It did not matter. The implication that he, a Chief Magister of Tson, would carry out such acts as were depicted on the walls of this house was beyond mere curse and insult. It was an act of treason against the Gver himself who had appointed Gahryll to such an august position. Only the fact that she was a woman stayed his hand from striking her. Instead, he turned to Mihiubel who was glaring in frustration at the woman.

"Seize her," he said, "And send men to shut this place down. We will see if there is any evidence of alkemya here."

He strode out the door without looking back.

The next day, as Gahryll was taking his morning quid of aslyn, Mihiubel knocked upon his door and entered his offices. He appeared not to have slept the night before. His eyes were red and his face clouded with exhaustion.

"What were you about? You look as though you passed near the Hall," Gahryll said, offering him a quid.

Mihiubel accepted the carefully folded leaf and slipped into his cheek. "I was searching the academy and following leads on the alkemya matter."

Gahryll frowned. "Ducaryh said there were no engines to be found there. No scrolls. No quicksilver element."

"Indeed," Mihiubel said with a sigh, sitting down in one of Gahryll's chairs. "I could find no trace either."

Gahryll spat into the spittoon at his feet. "Perhaps you were led astray."

"No, I think not. The man was quite insistent. He described the youth, he described the house, and he described all that went on there."

"Well, not all," Gahryll said and Mihiubel flushed. "At any rate, I see no reason to continue with this investigation. If evidence of false practice is found, then perhaps. But as it stands, this is an itinerant Enir of unsound morals and the Magistery will not be dedicating further time to this."

Energy seemed to course through Mihiubel's body, his exhaustion disappearing, and he leapt to his feet, crying out, "No, we must try. Let me speak to the matron again. A night in prison will surely have loosened her tongue."

Gahryll studied the Magister closely, his mouth filling with saliva from the aslyn. He spat again and nodded. "Very well. Speak to her. If she has anything to say, let me know. But this is the end of it, you understand."

Mihiubel bowed formally and hurried from the room. Gahryll leaned back in his chair, pondering the Magister and his strange fascination with this dead youth. Why, he wondered, did it matter so much—and clearly it mattered a great deal to Mihiubel—that justice be served in this case? People died every day in Tson without explanation or cause. There were murders and assassinations of people of all rank and station that the Magistery was helpless to solve. Each Magister accepted this as the lot the Gods had granted them. Up until this particular matter, Mihiubel had been no different and Gahryll wondered why that might be. What had changed?

He pondered the thought for a time, but came to no conclusion, and events soon drew him elsewhere. There was a riot in the southern quarter—evidently a Kragian merchant had somehow sparked fears that he was a Shadow Men agent—and he and a number of Magisters were called to attend to the matter. Normally the Gver's palace guard would handle such affairs, but so many of them had been drawn into the cohorts that accompanied the Gver into the desert to wage war that it now fell to the Magistery to ensure peace was kept in the city.

It was on towards evening, a slight chill seizing the air, the first sign of the changing of the season to autumn, when Gahryll at last returned to the Magisterium. He was sore and wearied from the day's efforts, stinking of smoke from the fires the rioters had started, and in no mood to think about the matter involving the Enir youth. Mihiubel was waiting for him at his door and Gahryll waved him away.

"Tomorrow, tomorrow. It can wait. I need wine and sleep."

"The woman has told all," Mihiubel said. "She has admitted there were foul practices there attended by Desecrators."

Gahryll sighed and beckoned the Magister into his offices. "And these were among the services she provided?"

"No," Mihiubel said, a little too quickly. "No. They merely used her rooms and the youths there."

"And she let them?"

"She felt she had no choice in the matter. They were important men, evidently. Nobles of rank. And she didn't feel she could come to us with this evidence for fear that we would throw her in jail."

"But now that she is in jail she will gladly implicate them." Gahryll threw himself into the chair behind his desk, sighing loudly and closing his eyes. He was really much too tired for this.

"Yes," Mihiubel said. He remained standing, shifting his weight from foot to foot. "She is reluctant to give me any names."

The Magister hesitated and Gahryll opened his eyes a sliver. "But she will if we treat her mercifully, I take it?"

Mihiubel nodded, looking down at his feet.

"If she cares a whit for her soul she would give us the names without hesitation."

"You cannot blame her. It is her life that she seeks to save now."

"Nor can I credit her. These Enir, forever negotiating." Gahryll sighed again, opening his eyes fully. "Very well. Let us go speak with her and see what she has to say."

They proceeded below into the bowels of the Magisterium where the prisoners were kept in low-ceilinged and cramped rooms, with only a sliver of a window offering any light. The place stank of shit and piss and rot. Gahryll winced as they descended below, shrinking away from the surrounding darkness, as though he expected the stench to imprint itself upon the fine silk of his robes. There were whispers, moans and grunts, of pain or pleasure—or perhaps both—Gahryll could not be certain.

One of the Magisterium guards led the way, carrying a lantern high above his head to illuminate the way for them through the damp stone lined corridors. He led them to the far end of the building to a large door, made of thick and heavy wood, barred with iron and locked with a key. As Gahryll and Mihiubel watched, the guard unbarred and unlocked the door, kicking it open. There was a sharp cry of pain and shouts of anger on the other side.

The guard yelled at them to move. "Up. Up. Out of the

way. Magisters to see the Enir witch. Where is she?"

The guard plunged into the dark cell, looking down at those who cowered at his feet and scrambled to make way for him. Gahryll caught glimpses of their faces as the light swung to and fro, their expressions shadowed masks, their eyes cold and empty. This was ostensibly the women's cell, but when numbers were high, as they were now with the unrest in the city, there seemed nearly as many men as women here. The guard found the Enir woman in the far corner beneath one of these men, who swore at the guard as he pulled him from her, and received a blow to the head from his cudgel. Gahryll was certain he saw part of the man's skull fly away under the blow.

He will not survive the night, he thought to himself. "Who is that man you just struck?" he said to guard when he arrived at the door, dragging the Enir matron with him. She looked dazed. There was blood on her lip and her one eye was darkening with the beginnings of a bruise.

The guard gave an elaborate shrug and set about locking the door. His indifference annoyed Gahryll and he had to remind himself he had come here for a purpose, and that was not to interrogate a guard over the minor details of his conduct. Those who resided here did so because they had committed wrongs in the eyes of the Gver, the Gods, and all Tson. What punishment they received, in addition to their imprisonment, was deserved.

Mihiubel took the woman by the arm and ushered her down the corridor. Gahryll followed behind, not looking to see that the guard was behind him. There was a gentleness to the Magister's gesture, a familiarity that annoyed Gahryll. No doubt Mihiubel thought it would make her more cooperative, but the Chief Magister still wanted to march up and push them apart, to have the guard put her in chains for her journey above.

It was only his exhaustion after such a long day that was provoking him, he had to remind himself. This matter was Mihiubel's obsession, let him proceed as he wished.

13

He would stand aside and observe and ensure that it was brought to a proper conclusion, whatever that might be, and whatever protests the Magister might offer.

They brought the woman to one of the rooms above the prison cells where interrogations took place. The dark implements of their trade were scattered throughout the room or hanging on the walls. There were whips and brands, pokers and pliers, a rack, and in one corner, some of their more terrible and rarely used devices. The vise, the pear of anguish, and other mechanisms for breaking and tearing at the flesh.

Mihiubel led the woman to a chair in the center of the room where all the implements were in full view, while Gahryll set about lighting the lanterns to fully illuminate them.

"You told me earlier that your rooms were used for false practice of alkemya and that you felt you could not deny the men who committed such deeds. Is this true?"

"Yes."

Mihiubel glanced at Gahryll, who had moved to stand to the side of the two of them. "This was because they were important men, I was given to understand. We will need their names so that we might investigate."

The woman closed her eyes and took a ragged breath. "I will give them to you on one condition."

"You are in no position to name conditions," Gahryll said, gesturing at the implements that surrounded them.

"I will give the man's name, the ringleader," the woman continued, ignoring Gahryll, her eyes imploring Mihiubel. "But if I do, you will set me free tonight. Now."

"Why should we do that?" Gahryll said, stepping nearer. He was irritated by her manner, her demands, and irritated at himself for interceding when he had told himself he would not. This was Mihiubel's cause, not his.

"My life is forfeit if I give you his name. He is a man of rank and considerable wealth. You will know the name I speak it. If I remain here, in this city, I will be dead in a fortnight. So I will give you the name, you will let me go, and I will be gone from this city."

Both Mihiubel and the woman looked at Gahryll, awaiting his decision. Their stares annoyed him as well, but he pushed that aside. He nodded to the Magister to proceed.

"We agree to your terms," Mihiubel said, unable to disguise the need his voice.

The woman gave the barest of nods and spoke only the name, three words that made Gahryll shudder.

"Bailad a Suher."

TWO:

DUTY

"WE HAVE TO question him. It is our duty as Magisters," Mihiubel insisted, for what seemed like the hundredth time that morning.

Gahryll rubbed his aching eyes and took another sip of dala, wanting to float away on a wave of its dark bitterness. After the prior days long struggles, he had returned home and drunk two flagons of wine to help ease his passage to sleep. The wine had served its purpose at the moment, but he had awoken exhausted and, most irritatingly, in considerable discomfort.

"Absolutely out of the question," he said. "I have indulged you in this matter long enough. The Asuher are friends of the Gver. They are friends of the Qraul, by all that is holy. We cannot simply march over to Bailad's estate and question him. Gver Hythel received him regularly. His family's treasury is paying for this mad adventure of the Qraul's in the desert. There will be consequences"

Mihiubel shook his head, pacing back and forth in front of the Chief Magister, his intensity barely contained. "The Gver and the Qraul are not here, are they? They are on their mad adventure. Consequences will be a good long

17

while in coming. In the meantime, we can expose him for what he is."

"And what exactly is he? A murderer? A false alkemyst? How are we to prove any of this?"

Mihiubel came to a halt in the middle of the room and looked plaintively at the Chief Magister. "I don't know. That is why we must at least speak to him. Get the measure of the man's robes."

There was no dissuading the man, Gahryll realized. If he forbade him from doing so, Mihiubel would simply call on the Asuher himself, alone. Gahryll could not allow such an unmitigated disaster to occur. The Magister was one of his best men, even if his passion, at times, led him to folly. He did not want to see Mihiubel throw his position and rank away over such an inconsequential matter. Not when he could be sitting in the chair Gahryll now occupied someday.

Bailad was known to be a dangerous man, long to hold a grudge. His purse was as deep as his reach was long. The Asuher in general were an unlikable family, given to endless machinations to place their favorites in positions of influence throughout the courts of the land. They were not above assassination, blackmail, kidnapping and torture to achieve their ends. It was Gahryll's opinion that they were as much responsible for the pointless and longstanding feud between the Apysel and Alastl as the heads of those families.

Such things were best not thought of, let alone spoken aloud, for no good could come of it. Just as no good could come of Mihiubel calling on Bailad a Suher to accuse him of being a Desecrator. The headache which had assailed him from the moment he had awakened, and had continued on through the morning, ebbing and flowing, returned now with a vengeance.

He knew he should forbid Mihiubel, and threaten him with a severe punishment if he disobeyed, but he could tell by the fierce expression on the young man's face that he would not be denied. Gahryll sighed. A dangerous man, Bailad a Suher, to be accusing of unspeakable acts. It would need a delicate hand.

"Very well," he said. "We will call upon him. As a courtesy. But I will ask the questions. You may attend, but you must not utter a word. And pray to Gods I don't come to regret this indulgence, Mihiubel."

Mihiubel looked as though he were going to argue, but a look from the Chief Magister stopped him and he nodded his assent.

"Let us get this over with," Gahryll said, draining his cup and standing. "I would not waste the day on it."

They journeyed first to the Suher House, which was not far from the Magisterium at the center of Tson. There they were informed by the second factor, a peninsular by his shade, that Bailad was at his estate, where he received most of his visitors.

"Would you please send word that we will be calling on him this morning," Gahryll said.

The second factor bowed and called for one his messengers, who was sent ahead of the palanquin carrying the two Magisters as it made its way through the city. Gahryll could sense the Mihiubel's disquiet beside him, his constant shifting irritating the Chief Magister. He turned to look pointedly at the younger man.

"I don't see why we need announce ourselves to the man before we arrive, Nes Gahryll," Mihiubel said. "We are better served by keeping the element of surprise."

Gahryll shook his head. He was already regretting giving into the Magister. The investigation would lead to nothing and he would be forced to answer for their interview of the Asuher at court. An unpleasant task, to say the least.

"He does not know why we are calling on him. All he knows is that we are. That is surprise enough for a man of rank, with the weight of purse to match his title. These things have to be handled with some tact. We don't want to be turned away at his gate."

"He must admit a Magister," Mihiubel said with force.

Gahryll simply shook his head again, not bothering with a reply. By the letter of the Gver's law, Mihiubel was correct, but the Gver's law was of no consequence to a man who could demand an audience with Hythel himself. The Magister did not understand such realities of the Realm. He was like a Cureder who thought the faithful followed the rules set out in his sermons. One had only to look at the dead Enir youth and his sordid life to see that not everyone obeyed the laws of the Gods.

Bailad a Suher's estate was in the Valin Hills district north of the Gver's palace, where most of the families of rank and wealth kept their homes. The hills overlooked the rest of the city, providing a natural redoubt to those who wished to keep those of lower standing away. They were also cooler during the warmest months of the year, maintaining a sort of spring-like temperature throughout the summer months. Even the Gver had an estate there, to which he would escape when the weather was at its hottest.

The Asuher estate house towered above the walls that surrounded it. Garhyll looked jealously at the gardened path, populated by fountains and statues of the gadarell— the spirit youths who accompanied Senteur on his journeys to the earth to lie with Melinon. There were flowers from all the realms, as well as peacocks and other brightly colored birds that he did not recognize.

The opulence only continued within the estate house, where they were ushered through the main doors to an entryway larger than any room in Gahryll's own house. At its center was a broad staircase that led to the upper chambers of the house, crafted from marble, as were the statues on either side at the bottom of the stairs. The Chief Magister did not recognize either figure and assumed they must be some important Asuher ancestors.

They waited as the servant left, hurrying up the staircase to fetch his master, neither of them able to stop gawking at the splendor that surrounded them. Even Mihiubel seemed cowed by it, the enormity of what they were doing finally dawning on him. Gahryll smiled thinly, turning his mind to the interview. He would ask some routine questions, not too probing, and see them quickly on their way. The Magister would let the matter lie and the youth could join those others whose cause of death could not be discovered and who were soon forgotten.

The servant soon returned, hurrying down the stairs, and bowed to both Magisters, informing them that Nes Bailad would be down to see them immediately. He did not offer them any refreshment, nor usher them to another room where the Asuher might receive them, which told Gahryll that Bailad intended their interview to be brief. The chief factor emerged on the balcony above a few minutes later, taking a moment to study his guests, before proceeding down the staircase to greet them.

Gahryll bowed deeply and formally, Mihiubel following his lead a moment later. Bailad gave a regal nod, his eyes narrowed as he studied the two Magisters, trying to gain their measure. Gahryll met his eyes briefly, and had to repress a shudder at what he saw there, smiling slightly in the hopes of setting the factor at ease. He was not at ease, could not be, given Bailad's unsettling gaze. It was as though he were a gadarell, or some other companion of the Gods, looking upon these mere mortals with utter indifference.

"How can I help you Magisters?" Bailad said. "I understand you have some questions regarding an investigation you are conducting. I am, of course, always at the service of the Magistery, but I cannot conceive of why you would need to talk with me."

Gahryll could feel sweat beginning to form on his upper lip and forehead. He inclined his head, acknowledging Bailad's words. "We must apologize for the

21

intrusion Nes Bailad. It is a minor matter, I assure you, and we bring it before you only as a matter of courtesy. We will not take up much of your valuable time."

He paused for breath, his mouth dry, wishing that Bailad had seen fit to offer them a drink on so hot a day. The Asuher gestured for him to continue, his expression unchanging.

"As I say Husem, an assuredly minor matter, but our duty before the Gver, is to pursue all such matters. To get to the heart of the matter, your name was mentioned in reference to an Enir youth who was found murdered."

Bailad raised an eyebrow to express his utter disbelief that something so inconsequential could be the reason for two Magisters to be present in his home.

"The youth, you see Nes Bailad, was a member of an academy. The proprietress told us that, not only were unspeakable acts being committed by the youths there, but there were in fact men engaged in the practice of false alkemya. She mentioned you as one such man. Now, obviously, this is someone desperate to save herself, and so I hesitate to bring such a slanderous accusation before you, but given its grave nature, I felt I must. If only to give you the opportunity to refute it."

Bailad's eyes narrowed until his pupils were barely visible as Gahryll spoke, feeling as though he were babbling ever more uncontrollably with each word. When the Chief Magister finished he paused to consider his words before speaking.

"That is a grave and slanderous accusation indeed Chief Magister. I appreciate your discretion in this matter. I, of course, refute everything this *woman* has said. The idea is preposterous."

"Indeed Nes Bailad," Gahryll said, wincing at the venomous tone of the Asuher and his odd emphasis on the word woman. It was as though he thought her, whoever she might be, no more than a beast to be culled from the herd. "I apologize again for even having to bring the matter to your attention. But as I say, we must pursue every connection, even one so dubious as this."

Bailad nodded. "This proprietress, this woman, I hope she receives a just punishment for spreading such falsehoods."

"Well, the, uh, investigation is ongoing, as I say. But rest assured we shall see punishment meted out as it is deserved. Rest assured."

Gahryll felt flustered and thick-tongued, as though he had spent the morning over a barrel of wine. His whole body seemed damp with sweat and he could feel it trickling down his head behind his ears. It was aggravating that he had allowed this man to so utterly intimidate him, so much so that he had now promised to investigate the proprietress who he had released the night before following his promise to her. She had no doubt already gone to the winds. And he was no nearer to finding out if there was any truth at all to her accusations of dark practices undertaken in the upper rooms of her establishment.

"See that you do," Bailad said, with a note of finality. Their audience had come to an end. He turned to go, glancing at the servant to let him know it was time for his guests to leave.

Before he could start back up the stairs, Mihiubel spoke in a loud voice, his words echoing up the staircase. "If I may ask Nes Bailad, what were you doing the night of the storm last week?"

Bailad turned around very slowly, his expression still. Gahryll felt a chill go through him and was glad that the Asuher's gaze was not directed at him. Mihiubel met Bailad's stare, refusing to look away, though the color did drain from his face.

"You may not," Bailad said in a low voice, enunciating each word with care.

He did not wait for a further response from either of the Magisters, turning on his heels and marching up the stairs. Gahryll watched him go, unable to stop himself from staring. His eyes followed the Asuher until he disappeared into one of the rooms above, even as the Chief Magister wondered what was compelling him. Turning back, he saw that the servant was glaring at him and he, not needing to be told, led Mihiubel from the house and the estate ground and returned to their palanquin.

They were both silent as the palanquin made its slow way out of the Valin Hills, both of them staring out the windows at the glimpses of estates. It was Mihiubel who broke their silence.

"Why did not you not question him about the false alkemya?"

All the warring emotions Gahryll had kept clenched like a fist in his chest during their audience with Bailad, his fear and anger, his embarrassment and anguish, burst forth at the Magister. "Why in the name of the Gods did you ask that question of him? The audience was over. I asked him and he denied it. There was nothing more to be said. Nothing more to be done."

"Nothing more to be done? You did not even so much as ask him a question, let alone interrogate him. All you did was promise to cover up his crimes."

"I did no such thing," Gahryll said. "If he has been slandered by this woman, who, I will remind you, ran a house of cock swallowers, then he is within his rights to ask for us to investigate. And we are obliged to do so."

Mihiubel flinched at his words. "There were acts committed in that house that you yourself said go against the very Gods, and yet you are unwilling to investigate."

"It is a house of cock swallowers," Gahryll said, surprised at his own fury. "They are soulless, worthy of any punishment they receive. They are not worth angering the Asuher over."

"You don't care at all about finding the truth of the matter here."

Mihiubel's anger was so great his whole body was shaking. The palanquin carriers glanced up at them, which told Gahryll they were both speaking much too loud. The whole street could no doubt hear them. He took a deep breath to compose himself and spoke in a quiet, even voice.

"I am willing to investigate. I have let you carry on for days with no evidence, beyond hearsay of those who would have no standing in any court in the Realm. I have let a woman, who I know to be guilty of abominable crimes, go free, and I have put my own rank and position at risk by allowing you to carry on before Bailad a Suher."

Mihiubel flinched. "You can't possibly believe him, can you?"

"It doesn't matter what I believe," Gahryll said, with what he hoped was an air of finality. "If there is no evidence of the false practice, then none was committed. We just have a dead Enir and a matron, who would do whatever it took to escape the justice owed her. Nothing more."

Mihiubel did not reply. When Gahryll glanced over, he was happy to see the Magister lost in apparent reflection. He hoped this would put things to rest. He had indulged Mihiubel as much as he was willing to. There were other crimes being committed, other forces of chaos afoot. They did not need to waste their time with this trifling matter. If Bailar a Suher had done some wrong, even Mihiubel would have to see now that there was little the Magistery could do about it. Only the Gver could raise a hand against him and his debts would weigh against that.

He sat back in the palanquin, observing their passage through the city, feeling satisfaction that matters had taken their course and that things would soon return to normal.

Two days following their audience with Bailad a Suher, the body of the proprietress was brought to the Magisterium. It was discovered in the alley behind the house she ran. Her body had been mutilated, her breasts gouged off and strange symbols carved upon her chest and stomach. A hot poker had been used to burn out her eyes and her wig had been removed and the hair beneath it sheared off. Her tongue had been removed as well, and when a more thorough examination was done it was found protruding from her vagina.

Gahryll felt ill as one of the Magisters outlined all that had been done to the woman. When the man was finished the Chief Magister asked him to summon the Chaziqs to see if they, or any of their shade, wished to claim the body. He suspected he already knew the answer. No one would want to be near someone who had inspired such ire in her killer. Nor would anyone in the Magisterium.

An investigation would need to be completed, and Gahryll determined that he would be the one to do it. No one else could be trusted to manage a situation this troublesome. It would have to be done quickly, with a suitable culprit found, or word would spread across Tson and panic with it. With the Veil active again, and the Gver and so many cohorts absent the city, any unrest could quickly become unmanageable. It would be his head that Cassahra, the Gvera, who ruled in her husband's absence, would seek if things spun beyond his control.

There was no doubt in his mind as to who had committed the deed, and that too meant a steady and discrete hand would be needed. Whether Bailad had been furious that a matron of an academy was speaking ill of him to the Magistery, or if he was seeking to cover the tracks of his own foul deeds, Gahryll couldn't say. There were striking similarities between what had been done to the proprietress and the youth, which suggested latter. It suggested a vile man, who had no care for the laws of the Gver.

All the more reason to ensure he did not find himself carved up similarly and left for dead in an alley in some godsforsaken corner of the city. To care about such matters and such people, as Mihiubel clearly did, was dangerous. It imperiled one's rank and position and, most importantly, one's health. Gahryll had no intention of risking any of those over the death of some depraved Enir youth or a proprietress of a foul academy.

With Ducaryh's help, a suitable candidate was identified on the rolls of those arrested in the previous two nights. A man of middling age and indeterminate profession had been accused of ravishing a dancer of the Midday after she and her companions had left a celebration at a noble's house. She had been badly mauled and left for dead by the man, but had survived and brought her accusation to the Magisterium the next morning. An investigation had been carried out, a suspect quickly identified—the man was apparently both well-known and well-disliked in his district, a dangerous concoction for a criminal—and an arrest made the same night the proprietress was murdered. The timing of the two events might require some finessing, but Gahryll was more than used to such matters.

As he was pondering how best to proceed with the matter—a letter to Gvera Cassahra outlining the quick work done by the Magistery on the matter, followed by a quick execution, seemed ideal—Mihiubel intruded upon his office in a state of frenzy at the death of the proprietress. Ducaryh was on his heels, apologizing profusely to the Chief Magister for allowing the disruption.

Gahryll waved his assistant away and turned to Mihiubel. "I will not hear anymore on the matter. As far as I am concerned, it is closed." He pointed at the letter he had begun to draft to the Gvera.

"You can seal the bodies in crypts as tightly as the Enir, but the dead will still rise up and walk," Mihiubel said, spittle flying from his mouth.

"What nonsense is this?" Gahryll said, frowning as he brushed the Magister's saliva from his letter.

"My apologies Chief Magister," Mihiubel said. "But we cannot allow this matter to stand as is. Bailad must be punished for what he has done. If we cannot get justice for those who have passed to Ulternon's Hall, we must at least stop him from seeing others join them."

"Neither of them will be found in Ulternon's Hall, I don't need to tell you," Gahryll said. "Perhaps their ancestors will see to them, perhaps not. Their living kind won't, that much I know."

"He is a monster. He must be stopped."

"Perhaps he is," Gahryll said. "If you have some evidence I can bring before the Gvera, to demonstrate why we are hounding one of her husband's most ardent supporters, son of one of the great merchant families of this Realm, I would ask that you bring it to me immediately. If not, I will continue with my letter to her about the suspect we presently have in our custody."

Mihiubel blinked in surprise. "Whoever that man is he is innocent."

"Of that murder, perhaps. But he will be broken on the wheel regardless. Adding another murder to his ledger will make no difference to the accounting."

"I will not allow that man to get away with all that he has," Mihiubel said, his fists clenched.

"You will," Gahryll said. "Because I am ordering you too. And because you value your life. A man like Bailad will have a letter prepared already to send to the Gvera, that will have you spending the remainder of your days in a cell, or worse. Your life is of no consequence to him and will not do much to lighten his purse. Please listen to me in this. We have to weigh our actions carefully."

"Your only concern is the weight of our actions. We have a higher duty, to order and justice and the Gods. I, for one, intend to see to it."

Mihiubel shouted these last words before storming from the room, leaving Gahryll staring out the door in disbelief. What in the Gods' name had gotten into the young Magister, he wondered? Theirs was not to fight for order and justice. There was little enough of each in this realm, so far from the reach of the Gods. All they could do was to fight disorder and chaos to some kind of stalemate and hope to keep a measure of balance in the Realm. To do that required that not all wrongs would be righted and that unjust deeds would go unpunished. Hard choices would have to be made, and Gahryll knew that he would make them.

That evening Gahryll retired from the Magisterium early, having dispatched Ducaryh to the palace with his letter to Gvera Cassahra and arranged the public execution of the guilty party for the following day. He returned to his own estate, one, which he would have been proud to tell anyone who asked, was more than befitting for a noble of the third rank. If the Gods smiled on him, his own children might rise to the second rank. His daughter might aspire to a marriage to an important family. His son might be appointed by Gver Hythel to a position at the court. Such things were well within his grasp.

He took dinner alone, as he often did, reflecting on the day, and then met with the head of his servants to review all that needed to be done with the estate. When he was satisfied that his affairs were in order he called upon his wife in her quarters, but was informed that she had left that afternoon to visit her parents at their estate west of the city. By their expressions he could tell they were either lying or withholding information from him.

Jehena had failed to mention any journey to see her family, but that was not unusual for her. She was willful in her ways and Gahryll had learned to accept that. He gave no more thought to it, deciding to retire to bed early. Tomorrow he would have his audience with the Gvera and the Master of Offices and he would need to be at his sharpest. He had no doubt his visit to Bailad a Suher's estate would be brought up and hard questions would be asked. The waters would be difficult to navigate.

He fell asleep almost immediately, slipping into a dream

where he wandered the halls of his estate looking for Jehena, who was mysteriously absent. None of his servants knew where she had gone and he could find no trace of her presence, even in her own quarters. Her robes were all gone and not a strand of hair could be seen lying on the covers of her bed or elsewhere.

For some reason, he was convinced that she must be present somewhere and he kept wandering through the corridors and in and out of the same rooms. After a time, he became aware that the estate had an additional wing, which he had somehow never set foot in. He began to explore it and was surprised to find himself in a vast space, the wing larger than his entire estate. By the time he came upon the magnificent staircase, leading down to the statues guarding the entrance, he realized he had somehow left his estate for Bailad a Suher's.

He did not dwell on how such a thing could be possible, he simply fled down the stairs and out the door before he could be discovered. As he tried to find his way from the estate grounds to the street, he somehow lost his way on the path and found himself in the gardens that surrounded the house. He tried to reverse his trail, but succeeded only in being drawn deeper and deeper into what he soon realized was a labyrinth, surrounded by tangled vegetation, which his gaze could not penetrate.

There was a house at the center of this verdant prison, which he recognized as the academy from the Enir Quarter. The proprietress greeted him as he entered and led him upstairs, though her eyes had been burned from her face and there was still blood dripping from the wounds she had suffered. She took him to a far room at the back of the house and stood aside, waiting for him to enter. Reluctantly, he did so and found the dead youth inside lying upon the bed. At his entrance, the youth leapt to his feet and walked over to Gahryll, moving stiffly, his body rigid from death, and drew him into his arms in a cold embrace.

He awoke to find himself covered in a sheen of sweat, the darkness around him absolute. Slipping from bed, he went to find a cloth to wipe the moisture from his body before a chill took hold. The dream still worked at his mind, the final image of his embrace returning to him again and again. The thought of it left him feeling disgusted and ashamed, the reasons for which he was not entirely sure. The dream was troubling on many levels, but the Gods did not send them idly. There was a purpose to them, a calling that he was to answer.

As he wiped his face dry, the answer came to him, like the pealing of a bell from a watchtower. He rushed to strike a lantern and struggled into his robes, calling out for his servants. One of them entered his bedroom, bleary eyed and unsteady with sleep. Gahryll told him to raise the carriers and have them ready his palanquin. The servant left without a reply, a dereliction of duty, which normally would have caused Gahryll to summon him back and excoriate him for his failure.

His own thoughts were elsewhere, though. As he hurried from his quarters, out to the courtyard where the palanquin lay, he glanced to the sky and saw the moon high overhead. It was deep into the night already, and it would nearly be morning by the time he arrived at his destination. He could only hope he was not too late.

The streets of the Valin Hills were quiet, but for the footsteps of the carriers and the odd creak that the palanquin gave as they carried it. They had met others as they passed through less noble districts to arrive here, but most of those had stayed to the shadows, wanting to avoid an encounter with whoever sat within the palanquin. Gahryll's hand had still strayed to the sword at his belt each time. It felt awkward sitting there at his waist. He rarely wore it, preferring a long dagger to defend himself while on Magistery business, but tonight he wanted something that would give a sterner appearance.

He had the carriers halt a street or two before the Asuher estate, in front of one of the rare drinkeries in the district. It appeared to be closed for the night, but an empty palanquin in front of a closed drinkery would attract fewer questions than anywhere else in this neighborhood. He went the rest of the way by foot, staying near the walls of estates where the shadows were heaviest. A dog barked for a time as he passed by one house, but otherwise the night remained undisturbed.

Once he was at the estate walls he made a careful circuit around to see if he could find Mihiubel, to no avail. It was impossible to say whether he had arrived early or too late, but he hoped it was the former. He needed to dissuade the Magister from his folly. He decided to wait just off the street, crouching by the wall, so that he could see anyone who approached, but would hopefully not be visible.

The air was surprisingly cool after the heat of the day and he regretted not putting on a warmer outer robe. He was forced to rub his arms and legs to keep them warm. As he was busying himself with that, he heard footsteps coming down the street toward the estate. By their number, he guessed it must be a palanquin with six carriers and moments later was gratified to see that he was correct.

At the head of the palanquin were two grim faced swords, both carrying lanterns hanging from rods aloft to the night, to guide the carriers. One of them removed a key from his robes and unlocked the gate, allowing the palanquin entry. Bailad a Suher was returning home then, Gahryll thought, hoping again that Mihiubel had yet to steal within his estate. The two swords let the palanquin pass, before locking the gate and heading to the house.

After the sound of their footsteps had died away, Gahryll heard another approaching, barely discernable, and he moved to intercept whoever it was. As he came around the corner of the wall, he could see a figure in dark, wearing dark non-descript robes and peering through the gate at the Asuher estate grounds. The figure whirled about, reaching for the sword at his belt, as the Chief Magister approached. Gahryll held up his hands, wondering if the other could see the gesture, or make out who it was.

"Don't be a fool," he whispered.

The figure went still in the darkness. "How did you know?" Mihiubel said.

"Because I am not one," Gahryll said, not wanting to tell the Magister about his dream and the message from the Gods. "Now come on."

He waved at Mihiubel with his hand, though he had no way of knowing if the Magister could see his gesture. Mihiubel remained where he was, turning back to peer through the gate, before looking again at Gahryll.

"I cannot do that," he said. "My duty lies in there."

Surprising both of them, Gahryll stepped forward and seized the younger man by the collar of his robe and dragged him from in front of the gate farther down the street where they would be out of earshot of anyone on the estate grounds.

"You cursed fool," he said. "You're putting both our lives at risk with this madness. If you go in there, there is only one outcome. And we both know what that is. We have seen it. Now, I have indulged in your whims for some time, but no longer. Now you are putting us both in danger."

"You don't understand," Mihiubel said, taking Gahryll's hand from his shoulder. "I've been following him all night. I've seen what he is about. He is practicing some unspeakable rites. The evidence we need is with him. I have to see this to the end. If I do, I will have what we need."

Gahryll shook his head in disbelief. "How exactly? Does he possess an alkemyc engine with his seal upon it? Once you remove anything from that estate, he can deny it was ever there and the Gvera and everyone at court will

33

believe it. All you will achieve is implicating yourself in his eyes. Think, before you ruin us both."

"You don't understand," Mihiubel said again. He paused, seeming to be ready to say more, before stopping himself.

"Do you think me such a fool too?" Gahryll said, allowing his anger and hurt to come through. "I understand only too well why my Magister is obsessed with a dead Enir youth and how he has made these connections between that handsome young man and that house of depravity, and from that house to the madman behind those walls. It was not intuition. It was not the hand of the Gods guiding you, was it?"

"It was not," Mihiubel managed to say at last, his voice heavy with emotion. "I knew Isahem well. He did not deserve what befell him."

"Is that so? What of your duty to the Magistery? To order? What of those things?" Gahryll could hardly keep his voice at a whisper with the anger coursing through him.

"He was a beautiful soul. I hope his ancestors found it." Mihiubel choked back a sob. "No one deserves what was done to him. And he was not the only one. Nor will he be the last. There is another young man in there now who will suffer the same fate."

"There was no false practice of alkemya in that house was there? You had that woman lie to me and she paid with her life."

"I knew you wouldn't allow me to investigate the matter further, unless I could find a reason that did not involve..." he trailed off and Gahryll could almost see the shrug of his shoulders through the darkness.

"To think I thought so highly of you. Give me one reason why I shouldn't have you thrown in a cell right now. You are as depraved as the monster you are trying to discredit."

Mihiubel reached out to put a hand on Gahryll's arm,

but the Chief Magister quickly brushed it aside. His panic subsided and was replaced by a growing sense of revulsion and horror. This man, who he had spent years working beside, who he had mentored and thought to be an honorable and decent Magister, one worthy of taking his place as Chief Magister when the time came, had shown himself to be something else. No matter what else happened tonight, he realized, Mihiubel could not remain at the Magistery. He was not a noble of rank and honor, worthy of the robes he wore.

Mihiubel seemed to sense Garhyll's thoughts and there was a finality to what he said next. "I understand that you disapprove of what I have done."

"The Gods themselves disapprove," Garhyll said with vehemence, but Mihiubel ignored him and kept talking.

"But know this. You have seen what was done to Isahem and Henia, but you do not know the true horror of it. I did not even truly understand until tonight. I told you they were unspeakable and I meant it. Whatever happens to me, and whatever you may think or feel, I beg of you, do not allow this man to continue with what he is doing. He is a desecrator truly. He must be stopped, no matter the cost. I am going to try. But if I fail, I beg you to remember the robes we shared. We stand for order, and we must stand against men like this when no one in the Realm will."

He was gone, slipping away into the darkness, before Gahryll had time to react. The Chief Magister turned to follow after him, knowing that it was his duty to stop him. All Mihiubel's talk of order was merely that; he was the one committing the crime this night. If he was captured by one of Bailad's swords—and he almost certainly would be—there was no telling what vengeance the Asuher would wreak upon him, the Magistery, and Gahryll himself.

Something stayed his hand, though he could not say what. Perhaps it was the Gods themselves, though in his heart Gahryll knew it could not be. This was his choice to let the Magister go and have the maelstrom that would follow visited upon him. He had called Mihiubel a fool, but it was he who was acting the fool now. His position and rank and all that he honored and held dear had slipped away in the darkness, going to his ruin.

Yet he could not bring himself to stop Mihiubel. He remained where he was waiting, hoping against hope, for the Magister to return. Only when the first glints of the morning light began to cast the shadows aside, leaving him nowhere to hide himself, did he return to the palanquin, his heart troubled and his thoughts in turmoil. By the time he returned to his estate a new day had begun.

THREE:

THE SACRIFICE

GAHRYLL WAS EXHAUSTED upon his return home and allowed himself a few hours of restless sleep, during which he was tortured by visions of Mihiubel's fate at the hands of Bailad a Suher. One of his servants awoke him from his agitated slumber to inform him a messenger had arrived from the Magisterium. Sick with trepidation, Gahryll hurried into his robes and went to meet the man. When he saw Ducaryh pacing back and forth nervously, he feared the worst.

"What is it?" he said in a brusque voice.

"You have been summoned to the Palace, Chief Magister," Ducaryh said, glancing behind him as though he expected the summons to be issued again from the very air. "By the Gvera herself. You are required immediately."

Gahryll felt his knees go weak and he feared he would collapse to the ground. He offered a brief, unspoken prayer to Melinon to protect her weak and unimportant vessel, and nodded at Ducaryh to lead the way. Awaiting them on the street outside his house was a palanquin with an escort of palace guards. The beat of Gahryll's heart felt unsteady and he found himself wondering if he would ever return from this journey, or if this might be his final opportunity to lay eyes upon his home. He nodded severely at the head of the guards, a stern looking man who did not acknowledge his greeting, and climbed into the palanquin with Ducaryh.

Their journey across the city was swift and Gahryll found himself ushered into the inner sanctums of the palace, with a rapidity and complete lack of ceremony and protocol that disturbed him. Whatever Mihiubel had done the night before it must have been grave indeed to demand this sort of response from the palace. He cursed himself again and again for failing to stop the wayward Magister. What had possessed him?

He was not brought to the great hall where he normally had his audiences with the Gver and all his court, and instead taken to a smaller room, in what he guessed was the Gvera's wing of the palace. She was already awaiting him, seated in a plain chair and wearing little finery. The Master of Offices, a brute and brutal looking man named Kahrwem loomed behind her chair, staring at Gahryll with disapproval.

Gahryll threw himself to the floor in obeisance as soon as he entered the room and rose, looking uneasily at the distance between he and Gvera Cassahra, thinking that it would be difficult, if not impossible, for him to approach further and complete the second obeisance protocol required.

"Let us dispense with ceremony, shall we Chief Magister," the Gvera said in a bored tone, beckoning him forward.

"Of course, Most Glorious," Gahryll said, bowing deeply and coming to stand before her. He stopped still some distance from her, unsure of how close he should come. Protocol and ceremony were much easier, he decided. There was no need for judgment, and no possibility of insult or mistake.

"Troubling news has reached our ears this morning, Chief Magister," Gvera Cassahra said, her intonation unchanged. "We have grave questions about the conduct of those in your employ and how you have acquitted yourself and the duties of your office."

Gahryll managed a nod in response, though barely. He felt faint, his forehead and neck damp with sweat, which only seemed to blossom more profusely under the glare of the fearsome Master of Offices.

"Bailad a Suher sent word to us this morning that you and a Magister presented yourself at his estate two days ago. Is this correct?"

"Yes, Most Glorious. It is."

"He said you made wild accusations toward him, Chief Magister, implying that he was a Desecrator."

"I did no such thing, Most Illustrious," Gahryll said, bowing as he spoke. "I was investigating a claim that Magister Mihiubel had uncovered that the Asuher was a practicing Desecrator. The witness was credible, though I doubted the truth of what she said. I wanted to give the noble Asuher himself the opportunity to respond to such a grievous accusation, you understand."

"This is babbling nonsense," Kahrwem said, interrupting Gahryll.

The Gvera held up a hand to quiet the courtier. "You say this witness was creditable. Who was she?"

Gahryll cleared his throat uncomfortably, feeling a fool for what he was about to say. "She was a proprietress of an academy, Most Glorious."

"You consider a woman of that poor quality to have credit of any sort. I question your investigatory acumen, Chief Magister," the Master of Offices said in a sneering voice.

Gahryll pursed his lips, trying hard not to glare at Kahrwem, who he found to be deeply objectionable. "I do, Most Illustrious. Oh, I have no doubt of her devious nature, and I do not mind telling you that the activities that took place within this academy were in contravention of all that is proscribed by the Cureders of this fine city. But she was no fool, and she was parlaying for her very life."

"More nonsense. Hardly to be believed."

"I did not believe it myself, Most Glorious. At least not as regards Bailad a Suher. But I could not simply fail to investigate the matter. She had very specific claims, and given recent history involving the Golden Veil, I felt I could not simply let the matter lie. Bailad met with me, as any honorable man would, and denied everything that she had said. He wanted her brought before the court under charges of slander."

"And was this done?" Gvera Cassahra said. Her expression had not changed a fraction in the entire time he had been in the room.

"Unfortunately not, Most Glorious. The Magister conducting the investigation was too impetuous. He thought to catch the false adepts in the act, so to speak, and so he had the proprietress released and set about following her. She was murdered before we could discover anything."

"By the false adepts?"

"No, Most Glorious. I believe my assistant delivered a missive to you yesterday. We have found the culprit in her murder, a man of poor quality, who ravished a dancer of the Midday the night before he murdered the proprietress."

"Are you aware, Chief Magister, that your Magister—this Mihiubel, I believe—paid a visit last evening to the Asuher estate?" Gvera Cassahra motioned to a servant Gahryll had not even noticed standing off behind her chair. She brought a cup of dala to her, which she accepted without taking her eyes from him. Gahryll found this unsettling for some reason.

"I was not, Most Illustrious," he said, unable to stop himself from staring jealously at her dala, the luxurious scent of which was filling the room, reminding him that he had not yet had his cups to start the day, after an evening when he had received little in the way of rest.

"I don't need to tell you, this is a grave breach of protocol, Chief Magister. Bailad a Suher wrote me this morning, asking that I inquire directly with you—he mentioned you by name—for he fears that he has become the subject of some sort of vendetta from the Magistery. I cannot imagine why that would be the case, given he is one of our most honorable subjects, but perhaps you can explain."

Gahryll swallowed. Mihiubel had failed in whatever mad design he had, and now it was clear that Bailad intended to extend his vendetta to him, if not the entire Magistery. He found himself wondering if he would be led from the palace right to the square for execution, or if they would conduct the deed somewhere within these walls.

"Nor can I, Most Glorious," he said. "I can assure you that is most assuredly not the case. As I have already stated, I was unaware of the Magister's actions last evening. I have no idea what Mihiubel intended by going there, but I can assure you he was not on Magistery business. Of that I have no doubt. We have found the guilty party in the proprietress's murder and as far as we are concerned, the matter against Bailad is closed."

There was a long pregnant pause, during which all manner of thoughts floated through Gahryll's mind.

"We will accept your assurances, Chief Magister, and hope they are true," Gvera Cassahra said. "We will inform the Asuher that we consider the matter with the rogue Magister to be a singular incident, not to be repeated. In the interests of ensuring that is the case, you will hand the matter over to the Master of Offices. He will conduct any further investigations, should he feel they are warranted."

With that, the Gvera rose to her feet and exited the room, as Gahryll prostrated himself before her again. When she was gone, Gahryll rose to his feet and was met by Kahrwem, who had moved from behind the Gvera's chair. The Master of Office's expression had softened in the absence of the Gvera and he put a large hand on

Gahryll's shoulder.

"You will want your man's body, Chief Magister," he said in a surprisingly gentle voice.

Gahryll could only manage a nod and followed the Master of Offices from the room. He was led below ground to where he knew the palace dungeon was, as well as its confessional instruments. Evidently, it was also where bodies were brought, for he was taken to a somber room, unfurnished, but for the table where Mihiubel lay. There was only one narrow barred window atop the room, hinting at a past purpose, so Kahrwem brought a lantern in, holding it aloft over the table so that Gahryll could see what had been done to Mihiubel.

It was a sight he would not soon forget. The skin had been removed from Mihiubel's face, but for his lips, which had been sewn shut around his penis. His eyes and nose had been gouged out and placed, Gahryll guessed, in his testicles, which had been split open and resewn. There were a number of symbols, arcane and strange, carved or burned upon his chest and stomach. Were these the same symbols that had been found on the matron and the youth? No doubt they were.

His hands and feet had been removed as well. Somehow Gahryll had not seen that in his first glance at the body. He had a sudden urge to scream, to throw his fists against the stone here until they were bloody. His whole body seemed to vibrate with rage and disgust, and emotions he could not even begin to define. It was overwhelming and he wanted to weep. He could feel Kahrwem's eyes upon him, so he worked to maintain his composure, turning to look at the Master of Offices.

"It seems the Magister resisted when confronted by the Asuher's swords. Unfortunately he perished in the resulting struggle. Would you agree with my assessment, Chief Magister?"

Garhyll met Kahrwem's gaze. "I see nothing here to dispute that."

43

Kahrwem nodded, as though Gahryll had passed some manner of test. "Good. I will release the body to you then. You will send any evidence you have regarding the matter involving the proprietress and the Desecrators to the palace by the end of today."

The Master of Offices left the room without waiting for a response. Gahryll remained with Mihiubel's corpse, being careful not to look upon it, understanding that this was a test of some sort, but unsure of what. Eventually Ducaryh appeared, accompanied by two palace guards. The assistant appeared unsurprised by the presence of Mhiubel's corpse and its horrific state. He produced a blanket to cover the body and helped the two guards shift the body to a gurney.

They made their way from the bowels of the dungeons to the gates above where the same palanquin and escort awaited them. Gahryll and Ducaryh were taken in the palanquin, with Mihiubel's corpse as an escort, to the Magisterium, where they were all deposited without ceremony. Ducaryh saw to the body and Gahryll went to his offices, calling for someone to fetch him some dala, wishing it could be something stronger.

The predicament he was in was severe, Gahryll realized, as he stared out the window upon the teeming street below the Magisterium. He had little evidence to present to the Master of Offices, and much of it would only serve to confirm his suspicions that the Magistery had been engaged in some conspiracy against Bailad a Suher. He could provide no evidence of false alkemya at the brothel in the Enir Quarter, for Mihiubel had conjured that from the atmosphere.

It did not matter, he suspected. The Master of Offices was not interested in carrying out a search for Desecrators hidden in their midst, he simply wanted assurances that the investigation would cease. Would that be enough to satisfy Bailad a Suher? Gahryll recalled Mihiubel's body, as well as the proprietress, and thought it very likely would not. Whatever he provided Kahrwem would be used against him, providing a pretext for the Gvera to arrest him. No doubt he would be executed.

These thoughts were like a solid dark pit from some poisoned fruit at the center of his stomach. All this could have been avoided if he had not surrendered to Mihiubel's demands that they investigate this Enir of no consequence. If he had set his admiration aside and refused to indulge the young Magister. Or if he had found the courage to stop him that night. The matter would have withered away, as it should have, and they both could have gone about their days.

Instead he had allowed himself to be seduced by Mihiubel. He had thought it was his investigatory tenacity, however misguided, that drove him to pursue his inquiries into the dead youth. Instead it was corruption of the worst sort. An infection of the soul. The Magister was as much a criminal as Bailad a Suher, and as implicated in the death of that youth. Isahem, Mihiubel had said his name was Isahem.

Gahryll shook his head to clear his thoughts. It did no good to dwell on what had been done. Mihiubel had been more than punished for his corruption. No one deserved to suffer that fate. He had to accept what the Magister had done and see to his own life.

As much as he detested the idea, the only path he could see forward was to continue the investigation Mihiubel had begun. He needed to give the Master of Offices a reason to proceed with the investigation, ideally one that would deflect the ire of Bailad a Suher away from Gahryll and the Magistery. He needed to conjure some false alkemysts out of the atmosphere, a feat worthy of an Adept.

He summoned Ducaryh. "What have you done with the Magister's body?"

"It is being prepared for the pyre, Nes Gahryll," the assistant said. "When it is ready, I will send word to the

Magister's family."

He meant, Gahryll knew, they were trying to hide what had been done to Mihiubel as best they could so that his family need not suffer further. He also knew that, as Chief Magister, it was his duty to inform the Ajorhkah of the loss of their favored son. On their journey back to the Magisterium, Gahryll had already determined that he would not do so. The honors of the Magistery would not be bestowed upon their son. He told himself that was because it would only serve to further raise the ire of Bailad a Suher, and in turn the palace, but in truth he knew the real reason.

"We need to go to the Enir Quarter," he said, wondering if his thoughts were visible upon his face. "No one can know where we are going. We don't want to be followed."

"I understand Husem," Ducaryh said, his own face impassive. "I will ready the palanquin."

Gahryll met him in the courtyard of the Magisterium, where the palanquin was ready with carriers in Magistery colors. They were taken on a circuitous route through the city, stopping at the Flower Market, one of busier markets in the city, where they exited the palanquin. The Chief Magister made a show of buying some flowers for his wife and they journeyed to his estate. The palanquin, with the Magistery carriers, left half an hour later, taking another circuitous route with several stops, before returning to the Magisterium. One of Gahryll's servants, dressed in Magistery robes, was on it.

He and Ducaryh changed into nondescript robes and slipped out the back of the estate, walking several blocks before hailing a palanquin. They had the carriers take them to the Enir Quarter by way of a convoluted path, doubling back on themselves several times. Only when Gahryll was satisfied they had lost any possible pursuit did he allow the carriers to go to Enir Quarter. He had them stop a street over from the academy house and he and Ducaryh made their way there via alleys, approaching from the rear.

The door was locked and no one responded to their knocking, but Garhyll had the apparatus necessary to pick it, acquired years ago from a thief he had arrested and seen imprisoned. He had become quite adept with the tools in the years since and he gained entrance with ease. The house within was empty and filled with signs of a frantic exit, a looting, or some combination of the two. Once word had come that the proprietress was dead, and the circumstances under which it had happened, her harlots would have feared the worst and fled, taking anything of value with them. Whoever owned the property would be waiting to ensure that the Magistery or the Palace was not about to seize the house before finding a proprietor to manage its affairs.

They found nothing of interest on the main floor, hardly surprising given its purpose as a pleasant facade to obscure the desecrating acts that took place above. There were a few rooms that might have been used for assignations, but they were, by and large empty, and the same proved true of the rooms they searched upstairs. There were beds and some larger furniture that were too difficult to move, though Gahryll suspected some of the more daring trulls might return for these too.

As they parsed the brothel's remains, Gahryll could not escape the thought that Mihiubel had been in these rooms and committed unspeakable acts in them. It made his skin crawl, and his anger at the young Magister returned in force. That he had to spend these frantic hours here, in a desperate bid to save his own life, because of that man and all he had done.

"What did you think of the Magister?" he asked Ducaryh.

"He was a good man," the assistant said, without looking up. "A good Magister. He believed. He did not deserve such a fate."

"No," Gahryll said. "He did not. What do mean he

believed?"

"In the Magistery. And in you."

Gahryll closed the door to the dresser he was peering in and turned to look at his assistant. "You don't know what kind of man he was."

"It is hard enough to know oneself, I would not claim to know another," Ducaryh said. "I know he admired you, as you admired him. And he trusted in you."

And I trusted in him, Gahryll thought, *and look what it has brought me.* "He had no soul."

"All men possess a soul, no matter how poisoned," Ducaryh intoned.

"Spare me your invocations," Garhyll said. He sighed and passed a hand over his head.

"There was some alkemya involved in his killing," Ducaryh said, as they left the room and proceeded to the next.

"How do you know that?" Garhyll said, coming to halt and staring at him.

"The writing carved on him. Those are Kragian letters. They are symbols the Desecrators used."

"You know what they mean?"

"Of course," the assistant said, bowing slightly. "I went north to fight the Desecrators with Gver Hythel, as you did. I worked with the Council Adepts after the war was over, looking for where the false adepts had hidden themselves. Because I knew the writing, I could read the symbols."

"And what did the symbols on Mihiubel mean?"

"There were some Desecrators who viewed their false practice as a faith. They believed Kercubegahedd was a prophet, sent by the Gods to teach them how to achieve balance in this realm."

"They know nothing of balance or the Gods. They threatened all that was balanced in this realm," Gahryll could not stop himself from saying.

Ducaryh shrugged, as though such theological matters

were beyond his understanding. "They carved these symbols on themselves to anoint their bodies for the ultimate sacrifice. They would be immolated by alkemya. Their alkemy and their very beings would be in service to Kercubegahedd and the Desecrators, and their spirits would be free to find their path to Ulternon's Hall."

"Those doors would be closed to them," Gahryll said reflexively, his mind already parsing what Ducaryh had told him. Was Bailad a Suher a Desecrator and follower of this stunted faith? He thought of his audience with the man, recalling his unsettling gaze. That was not a man who would sacrifice himself to the cause of others. He would demand sacrifices in his honor.

"Is the proprietress's body still at the Magisterium?" he said, another thought occurring to him. The Enir youth's would have been burned by now. Ducaryh nodded. "I want you to look upon it when we return there. Confirm that the markings are the same as Mihiubel's."

He was about to suggest they return there now and abandon their efforts here, for he was certain they would find nothing of use in the rooms that remained, when a muffled voice, speaking in the Renian tongue, stopped them both in their tracks. They waited, neither of them quite believing what they had heard, and there was another voice, indistinct, but unmistakably a response to the first.

"Where?" Gahryll said, and Ducaryh pointed to the far room at the corridor's end.

Gahryll strode to the door and threw it open, Ducaryh a step behind, revealing two Enir youths lying upon a bed whose sheets and covers had been removed. Both were unclothed and lay clasping each other's hands in what appeared to be a state of dazed bliss. The floor was cluttered with the same detritus that littered the rest of the house, though there seemed to be more of it here. There was a heavy stench of urine and feces that assaulted their nostrils as they stepped into the room.

Gahryll shook his head, trying not to gag, and muttered

a brief prayer to Melinon. The youths did not appear to notice him as he walked over to the bed. Their eyes were glazed over, the pupils frighteningly large, and they whispered in Renian to each other. They looked remarkably alike, he saw as he studied them more closely. He reached out to prod one of them on the shoulder and looked to Ducaryh.

"They have smoked some Harges flower, I would wager," his assistant said.

Gahryll nodded, turning back to the youths. "Wake up you two," he said in a loud and commanding voice. Their eyes both flicked over to him, a dim awareness showing.

"Wake up now. Tell me what you are doing here."

"Do you have the stamp for our coin?" one of them said, in a voice as hazy as their eyes.

"Never mind that," Gahryll said. "Tell me what you are doing here."

"He does not have the appetite for our banquet," the other said. "You should taste it. You have never known such delights."

"Do you know that we are brothers? How sweet a spoil that would be. And a bargain at the price."

"That is not true," the other confided to Gahryll. "The Matron told us to claim it."

They both giggled and lapsed back into conversation together, using their native tongue. Gahryll turned to Ducaryh, who shrugged.

"Why haven't you gone with the others?" Gahryll said, trying again, though he suspected it would be futile.

"He told us to remain here."

"He will come for us."

"Yes. He will sacrifice us on his altar." They both laughed again.

"Who will return?" Gahryll said, though he knew.

Neither of them responded and Gahryll turned away, motioning for Ducaryh to follow him. When they reached the door to leave one of the youths spoke, sounding dim and confused. "He has promised to scour us clean. Then we shall be fit to join our brother upon the altar."

Garhyll could not repress a shudder at her words, recalling the depredations Mihiubel had suffered. It seemed these two had been marked for the same fate. He turned to look at Ducaryh and saw that his assistant was uttering a silent invocation for their souls. Garhyll joined him and they returned to the streets and the palanquin.

FOUR:

THE DESECRATOR

AS THE PALANQUIN made its tortuous journey back through the streets of Tson, winding from district to district, Garhyll had ample time to think through his predicament and determine his next steps. He had gained nothing in his return to the academy in the Enir Quarter, except further evidence of Bailad a Suher's depravity. He knew far more than he cared to on that score. The Palace knew what Bailad was, or at least had some inkling, and they did not care. They wanted the Asuher coin.

Despair overwhelmed him at the inevitability of his arrest and execution, followed by a frenzied anger. He would not let these whoresons ruin him to protect some petty merchant.

He spoke to Ducaryh in a low undertone, so the carriers would not be able to hear him. "What do you suppose he is doing to them?"

Ducaryh thought for a moment. "He might be scouring them. That is what the Adepts did to the Desecrators we found."

"But one survives a scouring, yes?"

"That is so. It takes the alkemy and leaves only the husk of flesh behind. They are alive, but not as you or I are."

Gahryll considered this. "Why bother with the murder and torture then, I wonder? They would not be able to tell anyone what happened."

"Perhaps. It depends. But it would be dangerous to have scoured souls wandering the streets regardless. Any Adept who saw one would know and the Council would investigate."

Garhyll tapped a finger against his jaw, deep in thought. What Ducaryh said made sense. The Palace would not stand against Bailad, but the Council of Adepts most certainly would if they suspected him of practicing false alkemya. If he could somehow get the Council involved in this matter, he might be able to escape retribution from the Asuher and the Gvera.

"We need to find out what he is doing," he said. "How would we do that?"

Ducaryh looked out of palanquin onto the passing streets, reluctant to speak. "I know someone who might be able to help," he said at last. "He was a Desecrator, but he escaped justice from the Council Adepts. He would know."

Gahryll studied Ducaryh, a number of questions on his mind, but he put them aside. "He will help us, you think?"

"If I tell him to," Ducaryh said. "He is in my debt."

"And I would be in yours," Gahryll said.

Ducaryh nodded and nothing more was spoken between them. The assistant leaned forward to give instructions to the carriers as to where they should go.

The carriers brought them to the Eruh district near Tson's western walls, a dilapidated neighborhood inhabited mostly by criminal elements and those who associated with them. As they left the palanquin, Gahryll felt the eyes of the place upon him. He guessed there were few carriers that ever ventured onto these streets.

Ducaryh did not seem to share his discomfort, leading

him down what appeared to Gahryll to be an alley, but was in fact a street lined with hovels in various states of disrepair. There were few happy circumstances that would lead someone to inhabit the quarters here, and those of the man Ducaryh took him to seemed less happier than most. The straw roof to his building looked ready to fall in and there seemed to be grime and mold covering everything within. A man lay upon the ground in one corner, with a stained cloak thrown over his shoulders for warmth.

He did not stir as they entered and Ducaryh was forced to kick him in ribs to wake him. His face was dirty, as were his hands, nearly obscuring his Kragian extraction. He sat up, muttering to himself and looking confused, pushing a hand through his long, tangled hair.

"Fuihryn, wake up. Where is your head today?" Ducaryh said, his voice bitter with resentment.

Fuihryn blinked away the clouds from his eyes, his head bobbing unsteadily on his neck. "Where is your head, brother?"

"Enough. What have you taken? We need you sober and clear headed."

"Harges and mythres and all manner of things," the man said, emitting a rasping chuckle.

"Whoreson," Ducaryh said, shaking his head.

"She was your mother too," the man replied, laughing oddly.

Ducaryh sighed. "I will go get some dala."

He looked at Gahryll, who nodded. "I will keep him company."

Ducaryh left and the two waited, Garhyll standing in the middle of the room as far from anything as he could manage. Fuihryn stared glumly at his feet, not moving except to cough or clear his throat. Ducaryh returned a quarter of an hour later carrying three steaming mugs, handing one to Gahryll and kneeling down beside Fuihryn to force it into his hands.

The three men drank in silence, none of them looking

at each other. The dala was terrible, overly bitter and without depth, but it restored Gahryll. He had not realized how exhausted he was, after his ordeal the night before and his audience at the Palace and all that had followed, nor could he recall the last time he had eaten anything. There was a long day still to come and he needed to take care. He could ill afford mistakes or lapses in judgment and he was not so young as he had once been.

When they were all finished with their dala, Ducaryh turned to Fuihryn. "This is the Chief Magister of the city. I've told him what you are. He has some questions for you."

Fuihryn glanced from Ducaryh to Gahryll, looking as though he were beyond all caring. He nodded. Gahryll told him of the markings on the bodies and what else had been done, and their shared suspicion that false alkemya had been performed upon them.

"I looked at the markings Fuihryn. They were the same ones the Immolators drew upon themselves. What could he be doing?"

"Not Immolators," Fuihryn said, with a shake of his head. "They all killed themselves. Burned themselves up. Can't be them. The bodies are still there."

"So we gathered," Gahryll said. "What can he be doing? What rites is he carrying out?"

Fuihryn gave an exaggerated shrug. "Anything."

Garhyll sighed. Ducaryh knelt beside the man, grasping him by the chin to turn his head toward his own. Garhyll noticed the scars on his cheek, the symbol of the Thief drawn there, and the scars on his head where his left ear had been removed.

"Someone told us he intended to scour them. Those were his words. Could he be doing that as well?"

"He could do anything. The symbols only held meaning to the Immolators and they are all long dead. Long dead and gone. Those rites are gone. Their time is past." He sounded wistful as he spoke.

"Yes it is," Ducaryh said firmly and looked up at Gahryll for guidance.

The Chief Magister pursed his lips in thought, before draining the last of his dala. "Perhaps we are looking at this the wrong way. We know he is using false alkemya on them, what he is using it for is immaterial. They end up dead, whether from the alkemya or his tortures, but the Palace does not care about the dead. He will take care not to kill anyone who would make them care."

He had begun to pace the room without realizing it, Fuihryn and Ducaryh both following his peregrination from the corner of the room. "It is the Council who will care. They have orchestrated this war with the Shadow Men, they will not care if they rile the feathers of the Asuher. How do we make them aware of what is going on there, without implicating ourselves in the doing of it?"

He looked at the two Kragians for guidance. Ducaryh shook Fuihryn as though to wake him. "Answer the Chief Magister or I'll turn you over to the Council."

"You wouldn't brother, not after all these years."

"Perhaps he will not," Gahryll said. "But I will. Even if it means his life as well. All our lives are at risk. The Palace has me by the throat, so I will put the dagger to yours."

Fuihryn frowned. "I don't believe you."

Garhyll pulled the dagger from within his robes. "Shall I demonstrate my resolve? I see you have one ear still to give."

He took a step forward and the Kragian raised a hand. "I will keep my ear, thank you. He will have a number of engines if he is performing Immolators' rites, or something like them. But they will not be large ones, not if he wants to escape the attention of the Council. Any Adepts or Disciples in the city would sense alkemya being used on any large scale."

"How do we ensure that we gain their attention?"

"Someone would need to use them in a way that attracts their attention. Something big, something unsubtle."

"You can do that?" Gahryll said, gesturing with the dagger.

"Of course," Fuihryn said. "But why should I? I'd be putting my own life at risk then and not just my ear. I'd stink of alkemya just the same as whoever this man is. And my shade does me no favors."

"This man is the Gver's purse," Ducaryh said. "His family is the Qraul's purse, or one of them. They paid for the army that destroyed your kind and left you needing the kindness of a traitor to survive. Consider it your chance to exact some blood."

Gahryll studied the man's face, which still seemed dull from whatever he had ingested. "What do you say? We need a display that will draw every Adept remaining in Tson to this estate."

"I will bring the High Adept back from the desert," Fuihryn said, with a sneer and a bitter laugh.

"Very well. It is agreed then. We will do this tonight. I am going to return home and then to the Magisterium. I will need to send something to the Master of Offices. I trust you can see this man to the estate?" Gahryll looked at Ducaryh, who nodded.

"I will see it done, Chief Magister."

"Good. For this I promise that if we come through this fire, the Magistery will forget this Desecrator's existence."

"That shouldn't be hard," Fuihryn said with a broken smile. "You are looking at a ghost."

Garhyll looked at Ducaryh who nodded his agreement and the Chief Magister left without another word, hurrying back to the street to find the palanquin. The afternoon sun was already slipping in the sky. Time was short and there was much to be done.

Gahryll returned to his estate first, intending to say his goodbyes to his family in the event he did not survive the night. He was informed that his wife was still at her family's estate outside Tson. When he asked when she was expected to return he was met with silence and awkward expressions. Something was clearly going on, and the servants obviously knew what, but Gahryll did not have the luxury of time to inquire further as to what that might be.

Instead, he put that worry aside and called upon his daughter and son. They were both too young to truly understand what it would mean for him to never return after this night, so he simply wished them well and hoped that they would recall this day with some fondness in their later years. With that done, he donned his Magistery robe over the plain ones he had been wearing, though the heat made that extremely uncomfortably, and had his palanquin take him to the Magisterium.

There he worked with one of the notaries to draw up some documents reflecting the interviews Mihiubel had ostensibly conducted that led him to the Enir Quarter academy, as well as their interview with the matron where she accused Bailad a Suher. He finessed the wording of many of these, creating what he hoped would be the appearance of a network of false adepts, of which Bailad was implied to be a central player. It was a thin veil upon the truth, easily torn off, but he hoped it would be enough to spare him and the Magistery a closer investigation, provided he was successful this evening.

When he was finished he had one of his Magisters take the documents to the Palace. In the time remaining to him he attended to some Magistery business. All as he would on a normal day. As the sun set, he left the Magisterium, taking a palanquin home. Once inside the carriage, he slipped out of his Magistery outer robe, leaving it within for the carriers to deliver to his estate. The carriers found an empty street for him to slip out of the palanquin and into the darkness as they went on their way.

He made his way on foot to Valin, taking an indirect route and stopping for a bite to eat and to savor a final cup of wine. It was well after dark when he arrived and the streets were empty, but for a few palanquins escorting nobles to assignations in other parts of the city. He avoided the center of the streets, staying to the shadowed places, and secreted himself along the wall near where he had waited for Mihiubel the previous night.

It was hard to escape thoughts of the Magister as he waited for Ducaryh and Fuihryn to arrive. His mind was still unsettled on the matter of his betrayal. It was hard to see past his corruption to the man Gahryll had known and trusted. That man had been a lie, and yet he could not deny what Ducaryh had said. Mihiubel had trusted in him, had believed in the Magistery, and Gahryll had believed in him. Had wondered idly about his succeeding him to the position of Chief Magister. It had not all been lies.

Gahryll shook his head and steeled his resolve. It had been a foolish indulgence of a corrupt and depraved man, which had led to this dark pass tonight, where he had to face himself against a madman. The Palace was aligned against him and his life, and the future of his family and their rank, lay in doubt. All because of Mihiubel and the trust he had placed in him.

Footsteps alerted him to Ducaryh and Fuihryn's approach and he turned to peer at them through the gloom. They were hardly discernable, with only half a moon visible in the sky above.

"Any trouble?" he whispered.

"None," Ducaryh said. "And you?"

"All is well," Gahryll said. "He has not left for the evening yet. When he does, we will enter."

"How many guards? How many servants?" This from Fuihryn, who sounded nervous.

"He goes out with an escort, in a palanquin. I don't know that any guard remains behind, but we had best assume so. I imagine, or hope, that he keeps the servants in ignorance of what he does, so they will be in bed. How difficult will it be to find the engines?"

"Once we are inside I will be able to sense the alkemy of the quicksilver. I can almost feel it now." There was a need in Fuihryn's voice that disturbed Gahryll.

"The trick will be getting inside," Ducaryh said.

"I have the feeling that among us we have the requisite skills," Gahryll said.

He hoped that was true. In his own case, he knew well enough how thieves operated to understand the best to method to proceed by. He could only hope that Fuihryn's missing ear and scarred face was the result of a prolific career and not evidence of a miserable failure.

The same could be said for his skills as an alkemyst, but that was best not thought of. There were any number of things that could go wrong in the next hours and, as they waited for Bailad a Suher to leave, Gahryll had opportunity to dwell on all of them.

Bailad left an hour later, sometime after the bells at the Palace struck midnight. As with the previous evening, he was in a palanquin and accompanied by two guards bearing torches. They locked the gate behind them and darkness presided within, at least so far as Garhyll could see when he lifted himself up to peer over the wall. A nervous energy coursed through him, leaving him feeling weak.

Fuihryn had lay down to sleep while they waited and Ducaryh had to shake him awake as Gahryll lowered himself down from the wall. He put a hand on his assistant's shoulder.

"See us into the house from here and then go. There's no sense in you risking your life as well. You've done more than enough for me, and I suspect for him as well. Let us do this and save your position at the Magistery."

Ducaryh squeezed his arm in return and turned to Fuihryn. "I have suffered much anguish over you. What I have sacrificed only you and I need know. I am happy that you are at last using your false practices in a just cause."

"I curse you traitor, but I am glad that you have given me this chance," Fuihryn said, his voice warm and touched with amusement.

Ducaryh ignored his brother's jibe and turned to Gahryll. "He has a soul and it beckons you to see justice done as you must. Do not forget."

Garhyll was about to dispute what his assistant said, but thought better of it. He and Fuihryn watched as Ducaryh slipped away into the night leaving them alone. The moment, Garhyll realized, was now and the thought terrified him. His skills as Magister would be no help to him here. He was no sword, trained in combat, and no Adept capable of standing up to whatever Bailad was doing. It was one thing to investigate thieves such as Fuihryn, quite another to become one.

"Shall we," he said to Fuihryn, affecting confidence where he felt none.

The Kragian did not reply and it was a moment before Gahryll realized that he had already begun to pull himself over the wall. He scrambled after Fuihryn, muttering a curse under his breath, which was soon short from his efforts to keep up with his counterpart. How did a man, who by every appearance had subsisted the last fortnight on mythres alone, manage to move so quickly, he wondered?

They avoided the main door of the estate, moving around the side of the building until they came to what appeared to be the servant's entrance. Fuihryn tried the door and discovered that it was unlocked and they slipped within. How often, Gahryll asked himself, were his own doors left unguarded, because of the trust he put in his servants, a trust so often misplaced.

With Fuihryn in the lead they moved down the corridor at a quick pace. From what Gahryll could make out in the darkness, it seemed they were in the kitchens and servants quarters. Fuihryn made his way through the estate with the ease of one well practiced in moving through the darkness.

It set Gahryll's mind at ease, though he found it difficult to keep pace with the Kragian, given his own worries about stumbling into something in the darkness.

They walked for so long Gahryll began to wonder if he had become lost in another dream, until abruptly Fuihryn stopped in front of a heavy door. The lock on it was difficult and it took the Kragian some time to manage it, all the while Gahryll stood behind, checking over his own shoulder nervously. No one else seemed to be about, a miracle of sorts given the size of the household Bailad must retain. The house remained silent and the shadows still.

Fuihryn managed the lock, pulling the door open, as Gahryll murmured a silent thanks to the Gods. The door opened to a stairway that led below, though they could see only its first steps through the gloom. Fuihryn motioned for Gahryll to go first, as he reached into his robes. "The engines are down there," he said.

"We will have to risk a light," Gahryll said, taking a tentative first step onto the stairs as he tried to peer within the darkness.

Fuihryn pulled a slender glass cylinder from his robes, seemingly filled with quicksilver, for it emitted a haunting silver blue glow. It provided just enough illumination for them to see the outline of the stairs, if not what destination they led to. The Kragian handed the cylinder to Garhyll who was surprised at its warmth.

"Careful not to break it," he said. "Wouldn't want the quicksilver on you."

"We'll need to be quick. We don't want to still be down here when Bailad returns," Garhyll said, turning to start down the stairs.

"That is your concern," Fuihryn said, shutting the door behind Gahryll.

It was several seconds before Gahryll reacted to what had just happened, his mind refusing to believe it had taken place. He leapt toward the door only to find it could not be opened from his side, as Fuihryn had obviously realized immediately. It took all his self-control not to hammer his fist upon the wood and yell for the Kragian to open it. He leaned his head against the door and closed his eyes.

"What are you doing?" he said, in as loud a voice as he dared.

"I am leaving your fate to the Gver's purse," came the reply, in an amused voice. "While he is dealing with you, I can take what I please and make my escape with no one the wiser."

Rage spasmed through Gahryll's entire body. He had put his trust and his life in the hands of a thief. He, of all people in the Realm, should know to never trust a burglar. His hand was so tight around the cylinder of quicksilver he was afraid it would shatter.

"What about your promise to your brother? And your brothers in arms? Don't you want to strike a blow against the Gver's purse?" He was grasping at straws and he knew it.

"That time is long past and all my brothers are dead."

"Whatever your crimes are, I can have them pardoned. You no longer have to live in hiding." Garhyll was acutely aware of how desperate he sounded. He also knew it didn't matter. Begging was the order of the moment. "I can see this done for you, if let me out. I am the Chief Magister."

"Not for long," Fuihryn said.

Not by morning, Gahryll thought to himself, fighting back tears of anguish. How had it come to this? How had he been so led astray? Mihiubel, that soulless cock swallower, that daemon in fleshly robes.

He did not try to ply Fuihryn with any further entreaties. The Kragian had left already he was certain, going to hide himself and bide his time for Bailad's return. Gahryll offered a prayer to Ulternon, that he would ensure Fuihryn's discovery by Bailad's servants, so that he would be made to suffer as well. That led him to thoughts of Mihiubel, and the suffering he had endured, and he truly knew despair.

His anguish evaporated moments later, replaced by a renewed fury, and an all-consuming energy to find some means of escape from this predicament. Using the quicksilver cylinder, he peered at the door to see if there was any way he might be able to open it. The lock was on the other side and the hinges as well. It felt too heavy for him to break, and would be certain to rouse the entire house.

He briefly considered doing so anyway. The servants might have a key, and if they did, he might be able to convince them to let him out. Convince them that this was all some terrible misunderstanding. He was almost to convince himself, before sanity was restored to him. The servants would just leave him for their master to deal with, not wanting to raise his considerable ire, and Gahryll would suffer under his ministrations all the same.

Abandoning thoughts of the door, he turned and started down the stairs, offering prayers to Melinon that there was another exit below. The staircase was long, suggesting the rooms were vast and not some mere cellar for keeping wine. When he reached the bottom of the staircase he lifted up the cylinder to better cast its glow against the darkness, but the room he was in was so large he could not see anything of significance.

There was a lantern set on a hook beside the staircase and Garhyll decided there was little risk to his lighting it now. Once he sparked the oil, he slipped the cylinder the cursed Fuihryn had given him into his robes and looked around. The full extent of the chamber stretched beyond the lantern's illumination, but what he could see filled him with horror.

Scattered throughout the room were various implements of confession, but it was not these which disturbed the Chief Magister. At the room's far end, where the shadows still held sway against the lantern's light, the two youths from the academy were suspended in cages that pressed against their naked flesh. Beneath them were two alkemyc engines, their spirals of glass coiled like a snake preparing to strike. Beneath the tubes were pans, which Gahryll knew would be stocked with charcoal to heat the quicksilver and shift its element.

The Adepts spoke of astral and alkemy, of shaping alkemya from the shifting of the quicksilver through the apparatus. He understood little of such things. Or why the Adepts were so horrified by the use of the engines. Alkemya was alkemya to him, whether the fulcrum was a man or these contraptions. The power of it was monstrous, regardless of who wielded it, capable of rending a man's flesh and soul.

He moved nearer to the engines and the caged youths and saw that they both remained alive. They seemed barely aware of his presence, their expressions as absent as they had been before. The markings, which had been present on Mihiubel and the two dead Enir, were carved on their chests and backs as well. Blood from the carvings trailed down their bodies to the floor.

Gahryll reached out to touch one of them and found the blood still wet. These cuts had just been made, right before Bailad had left. If the youths were prepared, as seemed to be the case, for whatever nefarious rites the Asuher was practicing, why had he left the estate? Where had he gone?

He received his answer a moment later.

"Welcome, Chief Magister," Bailad a Suher said.

Gahryll whirled around, the blood going from his face, but he could find no trace of the Asuher. The room appeared empty, aside from the two youths and the engines. Was this some conjuring trick, some alkemya aided magic? Whatever it was, he desperately wanted to flee and had to fight the urge, lest he look a fool as he ran toward a locked door.

"You are earlier than I expected, though I am glad you have arrived. I have a fine evening planned."

His words made Gahryll shudder. He looked around the room, trying to find the source of the voice, but it seemed to be coming from everywhere around him. Behind him one of the youths shifted in his cage startling Gahryll.

"Are you a cock swallower like your Magister, I wonder? He claimed you were a man after his own taste. It's why he was sure you would come. It's why I left those soulless ones for you to find. I knew they would draw you here, so that I might drink of your spirit too."

Garhyll swallowed. His tongue seemed to have absented itself. Sweat beaded on his lip and neck, though the room was cool. He tried to think clearly. This was just a man, not some specter, and he needed to be prepared when he revealed himself. He pulled out his dagger. It would do him little good, but at least he would make the man defeat him.

"Nothing to say?" Bailad said. "You will talk soon enough. You should have heard how your Magister wept when I removed his stones. He deserved worse. It was a kindness in the end, I think."

"You're mad," Gahryll managed at last to say, feeling ridiculous as he spoke.

Bailad laughed. "The desperate words of a man grasping for his last moments. How pitiful. I expected more from you Chief Magister. I expected some potency to your spirit."

"I will play no part in your foul rites, no matter what you desire."

There was no response, the silence growing more and more ominous as Gahryll filled it with thoughts of what was to come. He heard the sound of hinges from a door opening, somewhere in the darkness where the lantern did not penetrate, followed by footsteps.

Bailad emerged from the shadows into the light. On

their initial meeting, Gahryll had sensed the terrible nature that lay behind his placid exterior. There had been something awful in his eyes, something beyond explanation. Now it was laid plain upon his visage, an absence of feeling, an absence of being. Gahryll could not put the thought into words, but he knew its horror, he felt the pull of its awful orbit and wanted more than ever to flee.

But there was nowhere left to run.

"Foul rites," Bailad said, grinning horribly. "The only foul part of them is the cock swallowers. Their depravity has no end, as you yourself should know in your line of work, Chief Magister. What I do is perform an act of kindness upon them, removing them from this Realm and restoring it to balance, as the Gods intended. Purifying it. And in return, I take their astral for my own. It is a fair exchange. A bargain."

"You are a monster," Gahryll said. "To even mention the Gods, given what you do here, is unholy. And what of this desecration you are committing with this false alkemya?"

His anger made him bold and Gahryll, clenching his dagger tight in his hand, took a step toward Bailad, who to all appearances stood alone and undefended. He was brought to a sudden halt after only two steps, his body struggling against some unseen force. For a moment he did not understand, until the nausea and his headache began. The air changed and there was a smell, unlike anything he had encountered before.

Bailad was seizing the astral of the room and twisting it into a seed of alkemy that he was using upon him, Gahryll realized. He had never been so close to an Adept before, even a false one, as the Asuher was. The power was terrifying.

"And I have not even begun," Bailad said, as if reading his thoughts.

Perhaps he was, perhaps the tales of his childhood

were true. Gahryll tried to open his mouth to speak, but was unable to. Struggle as he might, he could not move, could barely breath. The world seemed to be closing in around him, invisible walls pressing closer and closer.

The door above opened and there was the sound of footsteps on the stairs. Bailad turned away to look toward these newcomers and Gahryll could feel the bonds that held him momentarily relax. He had visions of running past the Asuher, up the stairway and out of the house. A futile thought, given the Desecrator would restore his alkemyc bonds as soon as he noticed Gahryll's freedom.

All thought of escape vanished as those descending the stairs came into view. The two swords, who had escorted the palanquin out of the estate earlier, emerged into the light, carrying between them the unconscious form of Ducaryh. They threw him to the ground at Bailad's feet and the assistant moaned softly, but otherwise was still. There was a trickle of blood coming from his nose.

Garhyll felt defeat then, utter and complete. With Ducaryh taken, and certain to suffer the same fate as he, there seemed nothing left to hope for. The Gods had abandoned them utterly. Anger surged in him again at the thought that no one would escape, that Bailad, a soulless, vile man, would be triumphant. He could not allow that to happen. His dagger was still clenched in his hand and Bailad was still inattentive.

Just as he readied himself to throw the weapon, Bailad turned, as if overhearing his thoughts again, and gestured to the two swords. "Disarm him."

The two swords stepped around Bailad and approached him from either side, drawing their own weapons. Gahryll threw his dagger to the ground in disgust. His expression must have betrayed his anger and shock, for Bailad laughed again.

"Watch them while I light the pans," he ordered the swords. "I want this finished by morning and there is much to be done."

One of the swords retrieved Gahryll's dagger from the ground and kept his eye upon him, while the other went to stand over Ducaryh. Gahryll looked from one man to the other, their unconcerned expressions infuriating him all the more.

"How can you stand by and let this man defy the Gods and the Gver's law? Have you no conscience? This man is a monster. What he does goes against every law in the Realm. And you are parties to it."

Neither sword responded, betraying no sign that they had even heard what Gahryll had said.

"You'll find no luck there, Chief Magister," Bailad said, as he busied himself sparking the charcoal in the pans beneath the contraptions. "These men are loyal to me. They understand the necessity of what I do. This city will be purified by my actions. The soulless and depraved will be banished, the cock swallowers served just punishment. Balance restored as the Gods intended. And if I should claim the alkemy produced by it, well that is a tax no different than the one the subjects of this city pay to Gver to keep their streets safe. And better spent, I would add, given the sorry state of our city under your watch."

"These are the ravings of a lunatic," Gahryll implored the swords. "Can't you see? Don't be seduced by him. The Council of Adepts forbids the stealing of alkemy from a living soul."

"The cock swallowers have no souls to speak of, only the spirit of alkemy," Bailad said. "A heady broth to be sure, one that I add to my own, where it rightfully belongs, at the heart of a man of standing and rank."

The charcoal was smoking in the pans and Gahryll could see the quicksilver beginning to respond to the fires below, it's silver blue color glowing brighter still and beginning to move through the carefully wrought tubes as it prepared to shift states.

"What possible use could you have for another man's alkemy? It goes beyond all bounds."

There was no dissuading the man from what he was doing, Gahryll knew, not now. And the swords had seen this all before and not raised a hand to stop him, so there was no help to come there. All he could do was hope to delay the inevitable a moment longer. Each second seemed precious, each breath more important than the last.

"The Council Adepts have such a limited vision of the realms of existence," Bailad said, warming to his audience. "They seek out reasons to limit their power, claiming the Gods forbid it. One cannot scour a soul they say. Yet, as soon as the Kragian Desecrators stand against them, what do they do? A scouring for all. I have no such hypocrisy. When Gods allow such power naturally, it is to be taken and used. And I will. Now let us begin."

He nodded at the swords and they both moved to pick up Ducaryh, who remained unconscious. Gahryll moved to stop them, but Bailad seized him again with his alkemya and he had to stand rooted to the ground and watch as his assistant was taken over to the engines. Tears stung his eyes and he emitted a strangled moan.

"Do not fret," Bailad said, chuckling as the swords stripped Ducaryh of his robes. "You will join your man here soon enough."

Gahryll responded with a frenzy of struggle, fighting against the invisible bonds that held him, until he was exhausted and wanted to collapse to the ground. The alkemya did not allow him and he slumped against it, surrendering to its terrible embrace. He worried for a moment that he had soiled himself, for there was growing warmth in his robes at his midsection, but he dismissed the thought. It did not matter, nothing did any longer.

The two swords had finished stripping Ducaryh of his robes and they pulled him to his feet, holding him by both arms in a fierce grip. They turned to face Bailad, who nodded in satisfaction and pulled a dagger from his robes. He readied it to inscribe the Kragian markings upon Ducaryh's flesh, before a thought stopped him.

"Give me the Magister's dagger. Let it be his weapon that draws his creature's blood." He turned to look at Gahryll as the sword retrieved the knife and passed it to him. "You should both be honored to be sacrificed so. Your alkemy will restore me better than any curative elixir. Does my face not look unlined? I shall be eternal."

"Why should I be honored?" Gahryll said. The warmth within his robes was growing. Was Bailad practicing some unseen alkemya upon his flesh already?

"How could you not be? Your miserable waste of a third rank life will be redeemed. You will perish, but your alkemy will live on within me, solidifying my being."

Gahryll gave a bitter laugh and Bailad looked confused, as though he could not understand how the Chief Magister could fail to understand the honor being done him. The sword had Gahryll's dagger and he passed it to Bailad, who stared at the Chief Magister. Gahryll could see dark and murderous thoughts in those eyes, and beyond them a yawning, terrifying emptiness that he did not want to contemplate. Bailad shook his head, as though to rouse himself from a daydream and turned back to Ducaryh, raising up the dagger.

As he did, Gahryll could feel the bonds that held him slacken. He tried to judge whether he would be able to throw himself upon Bailad before the swords intercepted him or the alkemyc chains were restored. It was a hopeless, desperate thought. His midsection now felt as though it were afire and he had to glance down at his robes to confirm that they were not in flames. What in the name of the Gods was happening?

It came to him in a burst of revelation: the quicksilver cylinder. Was it reacting somehow with the other quicksilver in the engines? Gahryll did not dwell on that question, stealing a hand into his robes just as Bailad put his first mark on Ducaryh's flesh. The cylinder scalded his hand, but Gahryll ignored the pain, pulling it free of his robes. He threw it at Bailad before he or the swords had time to respond.

The motion of his throw caught Bailad's attention and he turned to see what Gahryll was doing just as the cylinder arrived. To Gahryll's eyes it appeared as though it was going to pass by the Asuher, leaving him unharmed. Instead it burst, spraying quicksilver and glass into his face and down his robes. Bailad screamed, a horrible sound, and fell to his knees, clutching at his eyes. The swords dropped Ducaryh and ran to their master's side.

"I can't see," he said, in a pitiful voice, that changed a moment later to a rage filled bellow. "I'll see you suffer unending pain for this Chief Magister."

There was smoke coming from the quicksilver that coated him, and with it a strange and awful odor of burnt flesh and alkemy. Gahryll stared at the Asuher in horror, unsure what to do. His instinct was to flee, for the bonds that had held him had vanished and there was no one to stop him returning up the stairs. But there was Ducaryh and the two unfortunate Enir in their cages to think of. He could not abandon them to Bailad's vengeance.

The Asuher was apoplectic. He screamed at the swords to seize Gahryll and bring a cloth for his face, gesticulating wildly, all while promising eternal suffering for the Chief Magister. The two swords stood, drawing their weapons and moved toward Gahryll, who took a step back. Bailad abruptly went still, halting his ceaseless torrent of abuse, and looking up past Gahryll, as though he could somehow see through his burned eyes.

"There is another," he screamed. "Forget the Magister. Up the stairs."

The two swords glanced back at Bailad, a questioning look in their eyes.

Before they could do anything more, the fires in the engines burst forth from the pans, scything through the air as though possessed, to engulf both of them. Their anguished screams drowned out Bailad's own. He slammed his fist upon the ground, turning back toward the engines, as though to regain control of their apparatus.

Gahryll did not have time to brace himself before he was assaulted by waves of alkemy. He fell to the ground, bent over, as though facing a torrential storm. The power was too much to bear. His head ached with it and his stomach was overwhelmed with nausea. The smell of it was everywhere, surpassing even that of the burnt flesh of the swords. He was certain he heard thunder, the air pulsating with its calamitous echoes, but there was no sound beyond the deathly moans of the two men.

Bailad had gone silent, his face contorted into a terrible grimace as he fought an invisible battle against an unseen foe. Gahryll could see the change in his expression as he realized his defeat a moment before he too was engulfed in flames.

Unlike the swords he did not scream in agony. Instead, he seemed possessed by some daemonic energy. He somehow managed to raise himself to his feet and lurch forward, arms outstretched toward the engines.

They were on fire, the pans erupting, spitting glowing coals, the glass bursting and sending showers of quicksilver outward. Bailad was struck by the debris, but he did not slow, throwing himself into the growing conflagration of which he became an indistinguishable part.

Gahryll was thrown to the ground as the fire Bailad had embraced leapt up, an unseen furnace blowing air upon it, claiming the two youths in the cages. He gathered himself and looked up at their cages, praying to the Gods that they had not awoken before their souls fled their bodies. His eyes were stinging and wet from the smoke and he found himself coughing and sobbing. The fire seemed only to grow in force and through his tears he could see it nearing Ducaryh.

Fuihryn materialized at his side and dragged Gahryll to his feet. "Come on," he said, his eyes intent on Ducaryh. "He is going to send the whole place up before he dies."

They ran to Ducaryh, who lay upon the ground

coughing weakly, though he still seemed to be unconscious. Gahryll grabbed his robes and between the two of them they carried him up the stairs. The door, Gahryll was relieved to see, was open and they came out onto the main floor where a crowd of servants was gathering, clearly debating whether or not to risk their master's wrath and head below.

Gahryll called out to them in his most authoritative voice. "He's burning it all. Get everyone out while you have time."

There were, he noted as they moved toward the main door, no expressions of surprise on anyone's face. Everyone turned and left, without a backward glance at the stairs where Bailad was busy consuming all his work and himself. Gahryll and Fuihryn made their way to the gates of the estate, where they paused to help Ducaryh, who had awoken somewhat, into his robes. Fuihryn picked the lock of the gates, throwing them open, and the three of them went out onto the street and slipped away into the night.

One of the carriers announced that they had arrived at their destination and Gahryll started from his thoughts. He could not get the images of the night before from his mind. Sleep had been impossible once he and Fuihryn had brought Ducaryh to his estate where his servants could care for him. He and the Kragian had spent the rest of what remained of the night drinking dala in silence, each lost to his own thoughts.

Now he moved through the day as though asleep, seeing visions of the night before at the corners of sight, lost in a waking nightmare. He touched the summons from the Gver's Palace, which was tucked into his robes, above his heart, to remind himself that he was very much awake. The consequences of the night before were still to be played out today.

He had no sense of what Gvera Cassahra and Kahrwem would have been told about the death of Bailad a Suher, or how the Asuher themselves would react. Even if the evidence of false alkemya was incontrovertible, as Gahryll was certain it would be, it might be a politically necessary to remove the Chief Magister, who was at the center of the events surrounding the death of one of the Asuher. Better to sweep this whole mess away and pretend it had never occurred. A difficult thing to do with Gahryll still in a position of influence.

His fate awaited him, but he had decided it could wait a little longer. He had business to attend to first. He climbed down from the palanquin, asking the carriers to wait for him and went to the door. A servant opened it and took in his Magisters robes, his face falling a little before he recovered.

Gahryll nodded in understanding. "Chief Magister Gahryll a Tyranil to see Piyn a Jorhkah."

PRINCIPAL CHARACTERS

Asuher: important merchant family in Craitol. The Suher House is loyal to the Alastl and the Qraul.

Bailad a Suher: Head of Suher House in Tson.

Cassahra: Gvera of Tson, wife of Hythel

Ducaryh: Chief Magister's assistant in Tson

Fuihryn: brother of Ducaryh

Gahryll a Tyranil: Chief Magister of Tson

Henia: murdered Enir youth

Hythel: Gver of Tson

Isahem: murdered Enir youth

Jehena: wife of Chief Magister Gahryll in Tson

Kahrwem: Master of Offices to Gver Hythel

Mihiubel a Jorhkah: Magister in Tson

Piyn a Jorhkah: head of the Ajorkhah, noble family in Tson

GLOSSARY OF TERMS AND PLACES

Abapolly: mythical demon from Kragi

Ad Eselte: title of emperor in Renuih

Adept: practioner of alkemya

Aesen: canal in Darrhyn

Alkemy: the latent power within all elements that can be released by transmutation

Alkemya: the practice and study

Anchonites: monastic priest in Renuih

Ardeh: animal, raised for its wool, milk and meat

Asieren: Ad Ezern paradise in Renuih

Aslyn: leaf that is chewed

Astral: aspect of elements that contains alkemy

Asyl: psychotropic nectar

Ceinobyte: Renian priest

Celes: Ad Reteln paradise in Renuih

Chaziqs: leaders of Enir Quarters in Craitolian cities

Cohort: Craitolian amy unit

Corenedor: Renian officer in the army or Watch

Council of Adepts: ruling body of alkemycal practice in Craitol

Craitol: Realm of, as well as capital of the Realm; westernmost realm in all the lands

Cureders: Craitolian priest

Dala: beans, drink brewed from

Darrhyn: imperial city of Renuih

Desecrator: name given false practitioners of alkemya, particularly followers of Kercubegahedd

Devew: city and river in Kragi

Disciple: practitioner of alkemya, Adept's subordinate

Dravasyl: drinkery in Darrhyn

Elen: city in Renuih

Enir: a distinct religious sect of the Renian people

Enir Republics: once part of Renuih; now independent city states along the coast between Renuih and Craitol, south of the desert; inhabited by those of the Enir sect

Eresnan: River between Darrhyn and Sylaron in Renuih

Esyln: jewel of the Renian Empire in the desert; now a ruins inhabited by the Shadow Men

Fegh: city in Kragi Province

Gadarell: the spirit youths who accompanied Senteur on his journeys to the earth to lie with Melinon

Golden Veil: rebel group in Craitol, largely comprised of minor nobility upset at being denied status and position in the Realm.

Gver: Craitolian lord, governor of a particular territory

Haigah: mountain city on the border between Kragi and Craitol; a mountain pass

Harges flower: a drug to be smoked

The Hashil: central boulevard in Lastl

Hasierren: Lasisen sanctuary in Craitol

Hessen: Enir Republic

Hesite: district in Takyl

Hezier: ruler in the Enir Republics

Hueithel: neighborhood in Darrhyn

Hjai: second to a Vazeir in Renian Imperial administration.

Immolators: followers of Kercubegahedd. Carved Kragian symbols on themselves. Burned themselves alive rather than be taken by the Council Adepts.

Isinan: a street in Darrhyn

Jetthir: leader of a quadra, officer in the Renian army or Watch. Lower in rank than a Corenedor.

Kastril: Renian fruit

Kenir: coin of Renuih

Kercubegahedd: a failed disciple, leader of the Desecrators in Kragi.

Kragi: province in the north of Craitol; once an independent realm

Kulez: northern city in Renuih

Kylep: city in Craitol; seat of a Gver Byuvir

Lasisen: a sect of worshipers of Senteur in Craitol

Lastl: city in Craitol; seat of a Gver Keleprai

Lethle: city in Kragi Province

Luessan: one of the three eastern kingdoms that broke away from the Renuih Empire

Luisel: town in Renuih

Magister: officer of law in Craitol

Magisterium: building of the Magistery

Magistery: officers, or the office itself

Melinon: Craitolian god of the earth

Mgetir: island south of Craitol

Morning, Midday, Evening: factions in Craitol

Mythres: powder made from flowers native to Kragi

Nrai: port city in Craitol; one of the contestants in the Sea Challenge; seat of Gver Assuard

Nohritai: nobility in Renuih

Nuerrallah: one of the great sages of Reniuh

Qraul: ruler of Craitol

Quadra: unit of the armed forces in Renuih

Quicksilver: an element capable of inhabiting all constitutions simultaneously and decaying the astral of any substance

Pyrsedies: forts guarding the desert frontier in Craitol

Psyel: city in Craitol; seat of Gver Pervelte

Rakai: port city in Craitol; involved in Sea Challenge

Renuih: Empire in the east, former rulers of the desert

Sanader: religious authority in Craitol; usually has authority over a particular city or region

Senteur: Craitolian god of the heavens

Shadow Men: the people of the desert; also referred to as Shadows or by other pejoratives (demons, beasts, etc.)

Suliher: honorific for those in the Renian Watch or Army

Sylaron: major port city in Renuih

Takyl: city in Craitol; seat of Gver Duirhe

Tolote: coyote-like animal of the desert

Tson: city in Craitol; seat of Gver Hythel

Tuissar: Enir Republic

Uenam: district in Darrhyn

Ulternon: Craitolian god of the dead

Usgelt: city in Kragi Province

Vazeir: imperial administrator in Renuih

Watch: protectors of the imperial city Darrhyn

Xln: port city in Craitol, involved in Sea Challenge

Yuehilth: prison in Darrhyn

Yseltez: city in Craitol; seat of Gver Issilar

IF YOU ENJOYED
UNSPEAKABLE RITES,
YOU MIGHT ALSO LIKE:

REALM OF SHADOWS
VOLUME ONE OF THE SHADOW MEN
AN ALKEMYA NOVEL

Craitol and Renuih, two empires a world apart, divided by the desert that lies between them. A desert ruled by the Shadow Men.

An uneasy peace holds sway in both realms, hiding longstanding feuds and bitter rivalries. Until a Shadow Men raid on Renuih shatters the calm and sets in motion events no one can control.

Masiph id Ezern, unfavored son of the Imperial Vazeir, finds himself a hero following the raid. His father remains unmoved by his exploits and, in his bitterness, Masiph will find himself a reluctant participant in a plot against the empire.

As he finds himself drawn deeper and deeper into the conspiracy, he soon realizes there will be no escaping the realm of shadows, where intrigue and betrayal abound. And though the Shadow Men have gone quiet, they will not stay silent forever.

1

Clouds blanketed the sky, rippling bruises in the twilight. The city Darrhyn below, sprawling along the bend of a wide river, was draped in the resultant shadows, pierced only intermittently by the remnants of the day's sun. Hurried figures passed from street to street in certain of its quarters to light the lamps, while others were left to what the night would bring. Along the city's great wall the beacons in the towers were struck, signaling the changing of the Watch. The new quadras marched up tower stairs, the soldiers heading out to pace the ramparts, looking into the final glare of the sun as it cast the scrub of the desert in oranges and reds.

Within one of the watchtowers five men squinted in the lamplight at a just-overturned cup, none of them speaking. Above them the sentinel on duty was singing an academy song about a woman so light in her manners that she would invite any man to sup with her.

"Call," the dealer said as he removed his hand from the cup, its contents still a mystery.

The youth to his left exhaled slowly as he eyed the cup. "Even. Five kenir," he said, the flames of the beacon above them snapping as more oil was added.

"Odd. I'll see you, Husem," the man beside him said, and the youth grimaced. "You're too young to be a gamester, I think."

He had a face gone thick with age and a long scar that ran from his chin up to his ear, just above the line of his jaw on one side. When he grinned, as he was doing now, it had the effect of creating what seemed a double smile on that half of his face.

"He lacks ability," the dealer said.

"Short on talent as well," the man said, to the laughter of everyone but the youth. The others at the table followed through with their bets, all odd.

Masiph id Ezern bit his lip. "I hope this is all above board," he said, staring at the dealer whose hand had strayed back to the cup.

"I hope so too," the man, Achelluth, said. "Someone short on talent and without ability certainly can't handle the underboard of life."

Masiph bit his lip again, not replying, and the dealer pulled the cup away, revealing two dice—a four and a three. There were whoops from around the table, but he did not look up, his eyes fixed on the dull bones whose pips had betrayed him again.

"That's it. I'm out," he said, pushing the last of his coins across the table. "I'm getting some air."

"Neither the coin nor the stamp for it, Husem," Achelluth called out, the white of his scar almost gleaming. "You haven't run through your allowance already, have you?"

"Hardly. I have better things to spend it on than at this table."

"Well, at least you are wise enough to know you will be spending it here," Achelluth said to more laughter. Masiph just nodded and walked out the door.

He wandered from the tower, stopping just outside the glow of the beacon to lean against the ramparts. It had been a cool day, given the rains could not be far away, and now that the sun was nearly set the night brought a chill. One of the two men on patrol on this stretch of the wall passed by, and they greeted each other. Masiph reached into the folds of his robe for the pouch that held his aslyn and put a quid in his cheek.

"Quiet night," he said, as the soldier passed back in the other direction.

"Every cursed night is quiet, Husem."

Masiph smiled, starting to work at the quid, as he stared idly at the veil of the night descending upon the desert. Here, so near the Eresnan River, it was a green desert—the short grass and sage brush that was its hallmark, plentiful and vibrant in color and scent. Once the rains began there would be even more as other plants began to flower. It was something he was curious to see, for though he had lived in Darrhyn his entire life he, like so many others from the city, had not set foot outside the western wall. When he had travelled it had been east into the Ferryen Plains, or down the Eresnan where the desert, so near, was safely kept from sight by the trees that lined its banks. To most Darrhynna, the desert was worthy of no more than a wary glance to the west and a scuff of a boot heel at the earth when talk turned to the Shadow Men.

Masiph had joined the Watch at the beginning of the dry season, five months ago, over his father's objections. For once Ibrazol had relented, though it had not felt like a victory as Masiph had expected. It felt like his father had in some way outmaneuvered him again, achieving his desired end in allowing his son this. Perhaps he had. Masiph never could tell what his father's thoughts were and was still not clear on his own feelings now that he had achieved his desire. The work itself was tedious—a few weeks on, a few days off, and always a quiet night.

This in spite of what one could hear walking the streets. To listen to the talk there was to believe that the Imperial city's very existence was precarious, given its location in that nebulous region near the Empire's border where the desert began. And the desert was the Shadows' domain. Never mind that the Shadow Men, even as they were conquering the desert, shattering the Empire a hundred years ago, had never dared an attack on Darrhyn and its fabled great walls. None had in the five centuries it had served as capital of Renuih.

There had been a raid a week ago in Fardun, little more than a day's journey southeast—the first of the season, and earlier than usual, given the rains had not started. Strangely, the fact that it was an unimportant farming village seemed to lead to even more anguish among the populace. There was no sense to it, but why did there have to be? It was the Shadows, after all. They were without reason and purpose, moving like common beasts with the seasons, content with the barest of existences on the rock and scrub of the desert.

In the streets talk turned to conspiracy and invasion. This was the only tangible result of a Shadow Men raid. That afternoon Masiph had heard that the shadows were gathering near Ghehel and were working to rebuild the Nasuila Bridge to use as a gateway to strike at the heart of the Empire, cutting the Ferryen Plains off from the capital and the southern provinces. At any given moment in the rainy season Darrhyn was a day or hours away from a massive army of the Shadows materializing at its gates. In a week, maybe less, it would all be forgotten—until word of the next attack arrived.

We live in an age diminished, Masiph thought, *the shadows of greater days*. Before the fall of the desert, even during that desperate struggle to maintain their hold in that realm, the denizens of this city would never have cowered at the mention of a mere raid by the Shadows. The thought would have been laughable. Now those who had to memorize their invocations, and even some of their betters, spoke of the Shadow Men as the natural inhabitants of the desert. Generations of Renians had known no other life but that of the desert—and that included his own family—yet that seemed to be almost forgotten now, or at least dismissed.

"What's the thought this evening?" Nustef id Illied said to him as he stepped out of the tower. The Nohritai was older than his fellow nobleman, with narrow features and a heavier green tone to his skin than was usual for those from Darrhyn.

"We can only bear a life of fear so long," Masiph said.

"Heavy things indeed, especially for someone with no marrow in his bones," Nustef laughed.

"Where else do you find the pox but in the bones?"

"The voice of experience, perhaps? Are you preparing lines for your chronicle?"

"I don't think so. The historians just put whatever words they want into the mouths of whoever anyway. Husem Azyereh was illiterate, I've been told."

"Really?"

"Yes. He was not a favored cousin."

More laughter. "Fair enough, I suppose. I always forget that he had a life before he became the Ad Eselte's Vazeir."

"Someday though," Masiph said, "we'll have to do something about the shadows or we'll be nothing more than carrion for them to feast on. Better to act now than to be put to the squeak later."

"You shouldn't listen to what you hear in the drinkeries. It only bothers the blood."

"The drink or the talk?" he said.

"I wouldn't know these things. I lead a pious life, as my ancestors and the sage Delth proscribe."

Masiph spat over the wall in response and Nustef smiled. "Talk to Our Most Benevolent One. Don't you have his ear by now?"

"Oh yes, I join him daily for his constitutionals and we discuss all the important matters of the Empire in between verses."

"Does he really go walking about every morning?"

Masiph shrugged. I would be the last to know.

Nustef took his own quid out, putting it in his cheek, and the two of them chewed in silence. There was a small copse near the wall that was filled with dahrrynna birds, the capital's namesake, and their animated calls as they roused themselves for an evening of feasting on insects drowned the air. This was the scene that faced them every night as the sun slipped below the horizon, and that familiarity and the calm that now settled over the day's end was seductive.

Masiph felt strongly about what he said regarding the Shadows. It was an easy thing to be passionate about, given no one was so derelict of their senses as to invade the desert. A byproduct of the restlessness of youth, his father would say in that dismissive tone which burned his ears. That his father, and no doubt that useless philosopher Ad Eselte, frowned upon his views only served to confirm them even more firmly in his mind. Something would have to be done, if only because no one else seemed to think that was the case.

The last Renian force to invade the desert in an attempt to reclaim their birthright had been led by a cousin of his father's, Waleen, ten years before his own birth. Two hundred sons, the flower of the Darrhynna youth, had joined him, dazzled by his speeches calling for a crusade to purify the desert of the black scourge, to resurrect those ancestors lost there and restore the empire whole. The result was predictable: a laughable disaster guided by a mad fool. Most failed to return and those who did were ruined, never to be whole again. Masiph had seen a few of them on visits to other Nohritai homes, balding men who walked about like children, unsure of each step.

Such a catastrophe had the effect of ensuring that no Ad Eselte or Nohritai would propose a war against the Shadow Men for generations. Still, Masiph admired Waleen his madness. His cousin, he thought, probably had felt much as he did the echo in each step of his life. If a cauldron of blood in the desert was necessary to drag this plain into a new age, then let it come.

"He's a poet," he said, breaking their silence. "He has the pouting lips for squeaking after all. Certainly no stomach for war."

"Probably he's too concerned about self-important Nohritai who think they know better than him how to run the empire." Nustef said.

A clanging bell, not far down the wall, stifled Masiph's reply. They both looked at each other, not quite believing what they were hearing. It was an alarm. Darrhyn, first city of the Empire, was under attack.

2

The procession had lost any pretence of cohesion. People milled about drinking and watching various groups of musicians playing the sacred songs while dancers tried to keep time to the stumbling rhythms. Cureders took any opportunity afforded by a lull in the cacophonic orchestra to proclaim their day's sermon. "Be the light" was the ragged cheer that could be heard at the conclusion of any song, followed by some hoarse thoughts frantically put to voice on the need for balance in this disturbed era, before the musicians began anew. A woman, dressed in a mask of feathers dyed scarlet and little else, wandered through the procession, pausing at intervals to point skyward and let loose a curdling screech.

It was the third and final day of the Feast of Balance in Lastl city, and, as with the rest of the Realm of Craitol, the feast days concluded with a parade in honor of the Gods. What was unique in Lastl was the procession leader, which by tradition was a newly shorn ardeh. It all began in the morning at the city gates with Cureders intoning competing invocations throughout the crowd. The city's Gatekeeper led a group of representatives of the leading families of rank to shear the beast, still heavy with its winter wool. They were assisted by the animal's keepers, who worked with quick economy, squatting on the struggling creature and attacking its coat with flashing shears, while the noblemen stood by awkwardly, trying not

93

to get in the way, as some of the more exuberant of the crowd called them ardeh-biters.

As the wool was stripped off, it was carried by the noblemen to a fire of nashen wood and incense to be burned while the Sanader of the city and two of his Cureders chanted prayers to the Gods over it. The shearing complete, the noblemen helped roll the creature over, one of them getting kicked in the head, while the Gatekeeper ended up covered in piss to the delight of the crowd. A slap to its flank sent the ardeh on its way, darting forward with its strange, loping stride through the crowd. Cheers went up as it snorted and bucked, kicking an unfortunate few not paying close enough attention as it went by.

Nobleman and peasant, merchant and porter, mingled on the streets empty of litters for this day, people of all rank and class joining in song and drink. They followed the ardeh the rest of the day, the masked woman still shrieking, though by late afternoon she was reduced to little more than a dry croak. Hawkers went through the crowd offering food and drink and harder stuff, helping to restore the collective's strength.

With the day nearing its close, the crowd started to dissipate, the nobles leaving for celebrations at their estates, or, if they were fortunate in rank or connections, at the Gver's Palace, while commoners drifted off to taverns and music halls. The ardeh was left nosing about the streets for whatever sustenance it could find, with only four men remaining to carry on the procession. They serenaded the beast through the twilight, first with whatever sacreds they knew, then whatever hall songs came to mind, until finally, their bottles drank and their voices hoarse, they ran out of music and drifted off into the night.

•••

All the windows had been thrown open, so the scent

of the orange and olive trees outside drifted in on the gathering. A few had taken their cups and were out on the balconies, the better to appreciate the night air and the scents of the seven gardens of Jesieles for which the Gver's Palace was justly famed. The three of them had fallen silent, stirring the wine in their cups, when Ludenn noticed a tall man in soldier's dress passing near the door and called him over.

"Tysaras. Allow me to introduce you to two notables. Sedar, Chair of the Morning of our fair city, and Nes Asnen. Tysaras is a levied officer," he said to the other two, "assigned to the pyrsedies for how long?"

"Two winters. This was my first."

"Clearly a man of influence if you were able to get leave for the feast and an invite to the Palace."

Tysaras laughed. "Lucky in cards, I would say. There were two invitations for the officers. One went to the kehel and the other I won at the seconds' table."

"What was the game?" Asnen said.

"Five-card eycher."

"You sell yourself too short," Sedar said. "Eycher is a game of skill."

"You still need the cards to win, no matter your skill."

"A modest and intelligent officer," Asnen said. "All this time spent with Ludenn I'd forgotten it was possible."

"Just because I prefer to employ my talent in the laugh and liedown does not mean I am unfamiliar with loftier pursuits," Ludenn said with a smile.

"Yes, we know you spend most your days studying in Sedar's academies."

Ludenn shook his head. "Well, if I'd known all I was going to get was mocked, I wouldn't have invited Tysaras to join us. I had him convinced I was a man of respect and influence."

"So tell me," Sedar said, "what's life like in the pyrsedies? One hears such tales."

The young man shrugged. "There's some truth to that I

guess, but I haven't found it much of a hardship. There are hard men among the common soldiers, and the laborers are even worse. Really we're more magistery than soldiers out there, keeping the asylums."

"A poor place for an officer to be sent, I guess."

"It depends how you look at it. If you do well they look at you more highly than someone with a softer posting. For someone like myself, whose most influential friend is the illustrious Nes Ludenn…well, I probably have a better chance of advancing there."

"Oh, so this is how it is now," Ludenn said.

A pair of flickers in the tree behind them stirred at their chuckles. "In all honesty though, my young friend does not give himself enough credit. The pyrsedies are awful. The levied soldiers are a poor lot at best, mutinous at worst. All a result of our friend Nes Asnen and his like sending the worst of his that way. To say nothing of the laborers, who are common criminals at best. And the shadows and disease. It is the worst of the Realm. Any officer who acquits himself well there is worthy of honor."

Tysaras nodded in thanks to Ludenn. Asnen leaned against the balcony, "Have you seen much of the Shadow Men while you've been there? We keep hearing the border is quiet, but one wonders what that means."

"We've only had one attack since I've come on. To the south, especially near the coast, there are always more because of the Renian highways and the Republics. But the pyrsedies around us haven't had to deal with much. That may change with summer. I hear they move about the desert more with the rains."

"There was that one attack you had to deal with a month or so ago, wasn't there?" Sedar said to Ludenn.

"Yes, they somehow slipped past the pyrsedies. They were having a grand old time of it in the eastern estates when we came upon them. Almost got ourselves into a bit of trouble on that one, but we made out."

He started into telling Tysaras a story involving himself,

Asnen, and three dancers of the Evening, so Sedar excused himself to refill his cup. After the cool of the balcony the heat that met him inside was oppressive. There were no more than a hundred people in the hall, which could easily hold twice that, but the day's warmth and the humid bodies had conspired together unpleasantly. At the far end of the room was a stage where dancers and musicians sought to keep the wavering attention of those nearby. There was a troupe of acrobats to follow, he knew, as well as some actors to conclude the evening with the creation performance.

None of the talent was from the Morning; the Alastl had long been for the Evening and this Gver was no different. He would do well to keep an ear open to see if there was anyone that might be worth buying away from the other faction. The Gver was known for having a discerning ear for musicians, and also for his eye for dancers. If some of the rumors he heard were true, the Evening had to turn over half its dancers every season just to keep the Gver's interest.

He found an attendant who mixed wine and water in his cup and then decided to return to the balcony, although he knew he should be talking with any supporters of the Morning who were here to ensure that all his performers would be busy through the summer.

As he made his way, nodding and smiling at those he knew, a hand grasped his elbow and a woman said, "You've been avoiding me all night, Sedar."

"Not true," he said, turning and smiling. "I've been avoiding the heat."

"Oh, you poor thing," she said, a grin touching her lips. They were painted scarlet to match her silks, bringing out the subtler red of her skin to good effect. She was the wife of Bessu, a city magistrate and a loyal Morning supporter.

"Do you know Nes Rysseh?" she said, gesturing to the small man with owlish eyes at her elbow.

"Rest assured," Rysseh said, "I've been a Morning as

long as your husband."

"The Morning owe much of our success to both your families."

"I do hope that we won't be discussing the games," the wife of Bessu said. "I find the whole thing so tiresome."

"There's always time for that."

"What would you care to discuss?" Sedar said to her.

"Nes Rysseh and I were just talking about the rare appearance of the wife of Our Immortal Gver."

She gestured over Sedar's shoulder and he turned and saw Niriese ul Keleprai, surrounded by various ladies of the court, her face pinched and drawn. The conversation around her was animated, but she seemed withdrawn and distracted. Sedar watched with no little fascination as she turned to the woman speaking with a slight, confused smile. He had not, he was quite sure, seen her in over a year, and he regularly attended court functions. In that time he had heard any number of rumours as to her condition: that she had lost the use of limbs, that the ravages of the plague had left her face so horribly scarred that she refused to leave her quarters, or that one of the winter fevers had struck her and left her mad. All apparently untrue.

"Is this the first time she's been in public?"

Rysseh shook his head. "She was with Our Illustrious Keleprai at the Ceremony of Naming."

"I hadn't heard that," the wife of Bessu said.

"I was there. She did not look well. She looks much better tonight."

"Really. She doesn't look at all good to me."

"That day she could barely stand for the ceremony, and she didn't stand at all through the invocation. They carried her in and out on a litter."

Sedar pursed his lips. "You just wonder how long she is for this realm."

They all watched her for a moment, the gauntness of her cheeks, how drained they were of their natural red shade. The severe set of her mouth did nothing to dissuade their impressions.

"I wonder how she can display all the signs of rot and her husband none when the Illustrious Gver spends all his time beneath the arches of the Evening."

"He does take the road well-traveled," Sedar said. "Perhaps his badge has been enseamed with his house's rampant honor."

"That's awful," the wife of Bessu said. "I don't even want to hear any more."

Rysseh smiled and shrugged, meeting Sedar's eyes. "Well then, what would you care to discuss now?"

"Unlike the two of you, I have actual news, not just tawdry rumor. Bessu told me he has it on good authority that Our Most Majestic Qraul Laterala intends to allow Rakai to join the Sea Challenge this summer."

"Now this is news," Rysseh said.

"What brought this on, I wonder?" Sedar said. He had been to the Challenge once with his father and his ten-year-old self had thrilled to the sight of those huge vessels sweeping through Xln harbour. He had not understood what was taking place, the attacks and the feints of the ships, but it had been awe inspiring nonetheless. Especially with the crowd covering the entire docks, far greater than any he had seen at the games, even in the Qraul's Pantheon in Craitol.

"Perhaps our young Qraul has a reformist streak in him?" Rysseh said.

"Is he even allowed his own thoughts?"

"Now, my dear," Rysseh said, "I'm sure both the High Adept and Our Immortal Gver allow him some time for reflection."

"That is probably taken by his Qraulla, though I hear she is more salamander than wolf," Sedar said.

"It would explain why she has not risen yet, I suppose," the wife of Bessu said.

"I would hazard that she requires a heartier broth than

that boy provides."

A piercing giggle rose above the chatter of the gathering, leaving an awkward silence in its wake. The talk resumed, though a few amused glances were cast in the direction of the Gatekeeper of the city. He paid them no mind, cackling again at something one of his companions said. Although he had arrived after the dancers had taken the stage, he was already well into cups and was pale and sweating profusely, a sign that he had dabbled in more than a little mythres as well. His companions, all lesser nobility of the second and third ranks, were mocking him loudly, pointing to his sad appearance.

He laughed along with their jests, pouring back more wine as he did, but when he spied Gver Keleprai nearby making his way through the crowd he excused himself.

"Immortal Gver," he called, more loudly than he had intended.

"Noble Gatekeeper," the Gver said.

"Cousin. Brother."

"I would hope, Assyh, that I am one and not both. That would speak ill of my mother."

Assyh giggled loudly again, drawing titters of consternation from those nearby. "Oh. Yes. Cousin. Cousin, of course. I have a request, Most Immortal."

"Indeed."

"Yes, ah. It is, you see, my current office, Most Illustrious."

"Noble and worthy work."

"Oh, indeed, Most Gracious. Indeed. It's not that, of course. The work is, that is to say." He was startled by the loudness of his voice. But the goodwill of the wine rapidly overcame that and he found his way again.

"That is to say, Most Gracious, as much as it is noble work, I would most dearly like. And I feel my talents could be better used. Indeed. In another office, one more befitting of my rank. You see."

"Indeed."

"That is, ah, well, I believe, Most Immortal that, well, the appearance of a relative of the Gver does not reflect well on the office. You see."

"Do I need to remind you, noble cousin, why you were in need of such an unbefitting office?"

This elicited another giggle from Assyh and he fumbled with his cup.

"That is to say," Keleprai added, "I agree that someone of your rank should not be in such an office as Gatekeeper of the city."

Assyh flinched as if he had been struck a blow, his face going flush. "Do you know," he said, "that the cursed ardeh pissed all over me this morning? Some louts were calling me an ardehmonger in front of the whole city."

"These are the hazards of working with livestock, cousin. I'm sure in coming years these duties will weigh less heavily on you. I will take your request under advisement as well. Perhaps in some time I can authorize a review of your performance by the Master of Offices and we can determine whether you are worthy of reassignation. Be the light, noble cousin."

Keleprai nodded and then walked away, leaving the Gatekeeper standing alone, his mouth working silently while he passed his cup from hand to hand.

The dancers and musicians had retired, with acrobats taking their place onstage. Those nearby stomped their feet in encouragement as the troupe began with a routine on stilts involving flaming batons. As if on cue, attendants moved through the crowd with buckets of chipped ice for the celebrants to put in their cups or against their faces. There were several rooms adjoining the hall where couches were laid, along with trays of sweets and cheese. People began to gravitate towards them as if some signal had invisibly passed among them. Others sought places where they might taste some mythres or salen without any watchful eyes. And still others took advantage of the shifting crowd to slip away for more private assignations.

Most stayed in the main room and on its balconies. The acrobats, having doused their flames, were now engaged in a sword-swallowing routine and the crowd around the stage responded with more insistent stomping. A Cureder standing nearby, rattling in the wind, was exhorting his two companions on where he stood in several theological debates of the moment, with one of them playing advocate to his considerable frustration.

"Assuming we are formed in the image of the Gods, as they were formed in the image of the Nameless, then it seems clear that only one of the brothers Melinon drew to her side could have impregnated her, and thus humanity's father had to be either Ulternon or Senteur—but not both, as some would suggest."

"But why," the advocate said, "could the Goddess not be like the female wyle fish, which, as you know, collects the seed of many male wyles to impregnate its eggs? Isn't it said that all creatures were spawned in her loins? Like the wyle fish, we could have theoretically an infinite number of fathers."

"It does not even pass muster," the Cureder said. "One father is the only logical conclusion to draw, for surely the Gods are more alike us than some common, mouth-befouled fish."

It followed then, according to the Cureder, that the next obvious conclusion to draw was that Senteur was the father of us all, for Melinon would have clearly wanted to have a touch of the glory of the heavens in her children.

The advocate responded, with a deepening grin, that Ulternon was likely the chosen, for he was of the earth and the earth provided life, which was what the Goddess wished for her children. Or perhaps she was like those frogs and lizards, who, bereft of a male to mate with, are yet able to produce offspring. Then she might have more the aspect of a worm and have simply cut herself into an unending number of pieces, each of which became a living child. As she was unending herself, there was no need for conservation.

The actors were well into their performance by the time the Gver had finished circulating among his guests with well-wishing and he could allow himself some unwatered wine. He moved away from the stage, where the actors running their lines were competing with shouts from those in the crowd who desired another version, whether for aesthetic or theological reasons. Celebrants murmured and inclined their heads as he walked past and he nodded in turn. He had just decided to head for one of the other rooms for a sweet and perhaps something more when someone began to beckon for him.

"Nes Kigarle Vistuvyr a Nepene," he said as he wandered over.

"Most Sacred and Beneficent Gver," Kigarle said with a bow, "I thank you for gracing us with your presence. I was just informing my illustrious company of the triumphs of your youth."

"And yours as well, naturally," Keleprai said.

There were three others with Kigarle, a friend of the Alastl and his for many years. One was Nes Javiel of the Dyhens, whose father had been at his side ten years ago, along with Kigarle, when the armies had gone north to put down the Kragian uprising. His newly betrothed, Anisse, was beside him. Keleprai had stood for them at the ceremony only two weeks ago. The third was a young noblewoman who he vaguely recognized but could not place. Her hair was swept up, but he could not recall a husband or their families.

"Naturally, Gracious Keleprai," Kigarle said with a sweep of his hand in front of his impressive girth. "Do you know that these children, these sprites, know nothing of the gleaming reputations we possessed in our younger days?"

"Presumably we still do possess them."

"Speak for yourself, I should say."

"I should warn you, Most Immortal, that some of his stories could be considered treasonous," Javiel a Dyhen said with a smile.

"I have no doubt, noble."

"I was just about to tell them about our evening in Senteur's cloister. A fine story, but I thought you should be given the opportunity to defend yourself."

"I have always said it is your foresight I most value, Nes Kigarle."

Kigarle inclined his head in thanks and then turned to his young companions. "It was a summer night, many years ago, still early. A glorious night. There was a half moon, so we could make our way on the side streets without much difficulty. A perfect evening; it had been so hot all day and then the cool was so sweet, it was almost like a taste in the air with the ripening fruit in the trees."

"You are a poet, Nes Kigarle," Anisse said to him, and Keleprai snorted to the amusement of the others.

"But now, to the point," Kigarle said, lowering his voice. "We were in Nrai, a wonderful city if I may say. Why? I really don't remember. The Sea Challenge? I don't think it was that time of year, but perhaps. Noble Keleprai, do you recall?"

Keleprai waved his hand dismissively.

"You see how it is. Do you see? All these long years of faithful service and this is how our noble and gracious Gver deigns to treat me."

"Long years indeed," Keleprai said, and the three youths laughed. The young woman, whose family he still couldn't recall, touched him on the arm as she did, and he smiled at her.

"This discussion will clearly get us nowhere. At any rate, our Most Immortal lord and I, and several others, who will stay nameless for brevity's sake, because each of them has a story as to why they were there and so forth. Now we had been drinking obviously, we were young then, our beards hardly grown in, and a night in Nrai should not be wasted by youth. We had settled nicely into one of the finer public houses then, where the best musicians of the season were playing and various and sundry were about, including many about whom songs would later be written. It was, in short, looking to be an evening to mark. Alas, not to be.

"How can I express my sorrow, and indeed my rage, at what happened? It does not seem possible that we should be pulled from the establishment and into the darkness, but we were. And it was because our Most Immortal Gver was so insistent on the matter and brought it up continually. You see, unlike today, when he forgets things from one moment to the next, his memory had a lamentable persistence.

"It was, there seems, a woman in the city who Most Gracious Keleprai had at one time pursued. Who he was still pursuing. Now, she had been so terrified by his affections that she had hidden herself in one of Senteur's cloisters."

"As I recall, she was a student of astronomy," Keleprai said.

"Or perhaps her father had placed her there to protect her virtue from so scurrilous a youth," Kigarle continued without pause. "It doesn't matter. At any rate, we were treading our way towards holy ground.

"Now she had concealed herself in the cloister, but noble Lastl had some way or another—he had some contact among their Cureders, who knew what was going on, if I remember. So all we had to do was get him in there and whatever would happen, would happen, including, most likely, our eternal damnation. Of course, that would only occur if we were discovered, and Most Gracious Keleprai had a plan. The larger details escape me, and are unimportant really, but it was definitely not Mentirenius stealing into the keep in the dead of night.

"Ah, it comes back to me now. Don't laugh, young man, it will happen to you sooner than you think. We bribed the men on watch for the evening to look the other way as we scaled the walls. Oh, we shall be doomed to wander for eternity outside the doors of Ulternon's Hall for what we did that night. Regardless, we forged on through the various gardens of the place to the main quarters. The three of us were sentinels while Keleprai went in. Everything seemed fine. No one was up for invocations, and we were out of view of the observatory. But then he kept taking longer and longer to return. We started to get concerned. What if he had been discovered? What if the lady had called the guards down upon him? How soon would they be coming for us?

"It took him forever, but just as we were rolling some dice to see who would go up to look for him he came down and we made a graceful exit. All of us we returned to the city, aflush with the daring of our deed, and naturally we wanted the story. He'd spent so long in the room we all knew what had occurred. It seemed quite obvious. But Most Gracious Keleprai wasn't telling, which was most unlike him at the time. People in Kragi Province were versed in the intimate details of his life. Naturally, this only piqued our interest, and we were convinced that this would be the tale by which all tales would be measured. A story to be set to song.

"It took us until the sun was up, and we were all getting understandably a bit disturbed from the lack of sleep, but we got the story out of him. And I repeat it here for you now and insist that it never be forgotten. It seems Gver Keleprai had gone into the building, up the stairs and to the left, as he'd been told. Come right to her door, or at least what was supposed to be her door. He never did find out. Why, you ask, and well you should. Because the priests caught him in the act? No. *Because he never went in.* He spent the better part of the night standing outside the door wondering whether or not he should. As he said, 'I couldn't decide what to do or why I was really even there, and so I just left.'

"Now, I must say we were somewhat appalled by the whole thing and rightly so. We had risked our lives and our immortal souls—and I suppose we shall still see about that—and all for what? For him to stand at the door *and dither.*"

"Was it as he says, Most Illustrious?" the lady asked Keleprai to the laughter of the others, her hand brushing his again.

"He has the larger points more or less as they happened," Keleprai said. "I won't quibble them. I do seem to recall, though, that Nes Kigarle was so far gone by the time we exited the establishment that we practically had to carry him over the wall. Fortunately, he hadn't gained the stature that you see today."

The four laughed loudly, though Kigarle immediately began to protest loudly that he had taken only three glasses of wine on the evening, all judiciously watered, and anyway he wasn't so girthful now.

Another guest, Ussul a Vellar, a cousin of his wife's, pulled him aside and Keleprai resisted a grimace. No doubt, he wanted to ask for the favor of the Gver, just as Assyh had. Ussul was more worthy of honor than his cousin, a ridiculous, drunken fool, but he was still a youth, with little to distinguish him from any other noble of the second rank, beyond his relation to the Gver's wife. As Ussul begged forgiveness for his intrusion, saying that he only wished to speak of a position under the Master of Offices that he felt ideally suited for, Keleprai stared past him, his gaze fixed upon the young woman, who remained with Javiel and Anisse as Kigarle excused himself. She had, he thought, as he feigned interest in what Ussul was saying, the most wonderful eyes, almond-colored and alive. Remembering her touch upon his arm, he decided he would have to make certain to find her again before the evening came to a close.

REALM OF SHADOWS is now available.

ABOUT THE AUTHOR

Clint Westgard is the author of The Shadow Men Trilogy, set in the same universe as Unspeakable Rites, and the science fiction epic The Sojourners Cycle. In addition, he has published a work of historical fantasy set in colonial Peru, The Maleficio Chronicles, and a retelling of the Minotaur legend, The Trials of the Minotaur. Clint Westgard lives in Calgary, Alberta.

ALSO BY CLINT WESTGARD

Realm of Shadows
Volume One of The Shadow Men
An Alkemya Novel

Craitol and Renuih, two empires a world apart, divided by the desert that lies between them. A desert ruled by the Shadow Men.

An uneasy peace holds sway in both realms, hiding longstanding feuds and bitter rivalries. Until a Shadow Men raid on Renuih shatters the calm and sets in motion events no one can control.

Masiph id Ezern, unfavored son of the Imperial Vazeir, finds himself a hero following the raid. His father remains unmoved by his exploits and, in his bitterness, Masiph will find himself a reluctant participant in a plot against the empire.

As he finds himself drawn deeper and deeper into the conspiracy, he soon realizes there will be no escaping the realm of shadows, where intrigue and betrayal abound. And though the Shadow Men have gone quiet, they will not stay silent forever...

ALSO BY CLINT WESTGARD

Council of Shadows
Volume Two of The Shadow Men
An Alkemya Novel

Discontent continues to fester within the realms of Craitol and Renuih, fed by intrigues carried out in the shadows. As rivals and apostates struggle for supremacy, a long incubated plan begins to unfold.

Vyissan, a mysterious alkemycal practitioner arrives in Renuih, the latest strike in a long war over who shall control the secrets of alkemya and Craitol itself. He carries with him a secret that, once revealed, will reverberate across all realms. Before he can reveal it though, the conspirators against the emperor will strike their own blow.

But now, a new and more powerful menace looms on the horizon. The Shadow Men have gained the secrets of the Council Adept's alkemya and no one can be certain what they will do with it…

ALSO BY CLINT WESTGARD

Dance of Shadows
Volume Three of The Shadow Men
An Alkemya Novel

War with the Shadow Men looms in both realms as the
consequences of the Gvers' Council in Craitol begin to
make themselves known. A war that could end in glorious
triumph or bitter disaster.

Doubt shadows everyone's steps, for they know there are
no certainties in the desert. Especially now the Shadow
Men have made the art of alkemya their own.

No one has more questions than Vyissan, for he is
working in service to a cause he is no longer sure he
believes in. And now he must undertake a journey with
those who both loathe and fear him. Before the first sword
is drawn, his life will be under threat.

But his will not be the only one, for somewhere in the
desert the Shadow Men lie in wait...

ALSO BY CLINT WESTGARD

The Forgotten
Volume One of The Sojourners Cycle

Who is David Aeida? And what does he know that has so
many people pursuing him?

David doesn't know. He can't remember anything about
who he is. But he finds himself ensnared in a vicious
conflict between a religious cult and a guild that patrols the
crossings between multiple universes. They will both stop
at nothing to gain whatever knowledge he possesses. Most
dangerous of all, is the implacable hunter, known only as
the Seeker, who has his own reasons for wanting to find
David.

His only hope is to recover his memories before they do.
His only ally is a woman named Meredith, and she
definitely knows more than she is telling...

Spanning both universes and the human mind, The
Forgotten is an unforgettable science fiction thriller that
questions the very nature of identity. It is the first volume
of the Sojourners Cycle, an epic that will encompass the
fates of universes and humanity itself.

ALSO BY CLINT WESTGARD

The Apostate
Volume Two of The Sojourners Cycle

Laila has only one goal in mind. To have her revenge upon the Grand Regent for all he has done to her. First, though, she needs to find her way across the universes.

That is easier said than done. The Grand Regent's agents are still pursuing her. As is the Society of Travellers. And the Seeker lurks somewhere, waiting for his moment to strike.

Laila has a plan, though, and a few tricks of her own. But she will discover that not everything is at seems. For the war she has given her life to hides a far greater conflict.

Spanning multiple universes and the complexities of the human mind, The Apostate, continues the incredible journey begun in The Forgotten. The second volume of The Sojourners Cycle is an unforgettable science fiction epic that encompasses the fates of universes and humanity itself.

ALSO BY CLINT WESTGARD

The Acolyte
Volume Three of The Sojourners Cycle

After crossing the universes to join with Toma Osahi's
group of renegades in their battle for control of the
Church of Regents, Laila finds herself in a precarious
position. While they both share the same goal—the
destruction of the Grand Regent—Osahi doesn't know
who Laila really is. What will he do if he finds out?

While Laila struggles to keep her identity secret, Osahi and
his people pull her deeper and deeper into a search for
Ana that promises to shed light on the dark secrets of the
Watchers' Order and the Acolytes. Before she can find
those answers though, Laila will have to face what lies
within.

Crossing the universes has unsettled the already shaky
equilibrium in her mind. If she wants to return herself to
her own body, she will have to act fast, for the
consequences of what Acolytes did to her are still
reverberating. And Aeida hides somewhere, waiting for his
time to come.

The thrilling third volume of the Sojourners Cycle
continues Laila's incredible journey across the universes
against incredible odds, as well as exploring her past,
including the pivotal role she played in the rise of the
Grand Regent and her own downfall at his hands.

ALSO BY CLINT WESTGARD

The Double
Volume Four of The Sojourners Cycle

David Aeida now commands his body, having cast Laila aside. He has sworn fealty to the Grand Regent, who wants him by his side and sees that his loyalty is rewarded.

But the Grand Regent is not the man he was. He is paranoid and suspicious of everyone, isolated in his tower, and thirsting for vengeance against those he feels have wronged him. How long until he turns on Aeida as well?

That is only the beginning of Aeida's problems. For he knows the Seeker and the Society of Travelers remain to play their parts. Both desire nothing more than the utter destruction of the Church of Regents and all its works. And though Laila has been defeated, he knows better than anyone not to assume she has been vanquished.

The epic fourth volume of the Sojourners Cycle centers upon the many betrayals and lies at the heart of the faith of the Church of Regents and the devastation upon the lives of the faithful they have wrought. Desire and guilt, love and revenge, rage and despair will drive them all, with consequences for all the universes.

ALSO BY CLINT WESTGARD

The Sojourner
Volume Five of The Sojourners Cycle

Laila's strange and reluctant alliance with the Seeker
continues, though she does not know where it will lead
her. She fears it will place her in another prison, worse
than the one she has just managed to escape.

But her escape is not entirely complete. For though she
has been restored to her own flesh, parts of Aeida
somehow still remain. Along with some other she does not
recognize. Is this some aftereffect of the Acolyte's bizarre
procedure? Or the result of the Seeker's meddling?

All this pales in comparison to what Laila soon discovers.
That she has an unwanted part to play in an ancient
struggle for who will rule the crossings between the
universes and all that lies in them.

In the stunning conclusion to the Sojourners Cycle Laila
will be faced with a terrible choice, one that will decide her
fate and humanity's.

ALSO BY CLINT WESTGARD

The Maleficio Chronicles

Luisa is always more than she appears. Rumor and mystery surround her. And strange events seem to follow wherever she goes.

Born in Lima, City of Kings, to a noble family, her father so fears her true nature that he banishes her to a convent. There she falls under the suspicion of the Inquisition and decides to flee.

Disguised as a man, she embarks upon a series of wild adventures, dueling, carousing, and gambling her way across colonial Peru. But everything changes when someone recognizes her for what she truly is, and soon she finds herself fighting for her very survival.

In a world where she will always stand apart, Luisa undergoes a strange journey, marked by betrayal and murder, terrible powers and mysterious strangers. *The Maleficio Chronicles* is her incredible confession and a story like no other.

ALSO BY CLINT WESTGARD

The Trials of the Minotaur

In the fifth year of the rule of Auten the One Eyed a minotaur is born to one of Colosi's most important families.

Taken from his mother as a newborn, exiled and cast from his family, the minotaur vows to return to the imperial city and take his rightful place as a patrician in the empire. But the patriarch of the family, his grandfather, will stop at nothing to see this blemish to his honor destroyed.

And so begins an epic journey, through lands beyond imagining, marked by despair and exile, triumph and betrayal. At its heart lies a quest to be free.